# THE MEAN GIRL

## ASHLEY ROSE

*Huge thanks to Jodi Kozlowski and Book Nerdy*

# FOREWORD

Want to be first to hear about specials on Ashley Rose books? Sign up
for her newsletter
https://www.subscribepage.com/ashleyrosebooks
and receive the exclusive epilogue to her young adult mystery, Raven.
**You'll also be the first to know when each book in the Pacific High
Series is available!**

# 1

Balboa Beach

Spring is in the air with a vengeance and it looks like the entire student body of Pacific High is on the beach tonight huddled around a series of bonfires lining the sand.

Holding Hunter's hand, I smile up at him. His face is illuminated by the orange glow. Firelight flickers in his eyes as he gazes down at me and I'm taken aback by the look I see there.

I've never seen love in anyone else's eyes—except my own mother.

He loves me. And he's said it out loud. But seeing the look in his eyes, is a powerful and heady feeling. It sends a surge of affection and exhilaration through me. At the same time, it's terrifying.

Because it feels tenuous.

As if it could go away any day.

High school is almost over. College could change everything. And while it's probably realistic to realize that my relationship with Hunter could very well have an expiration date, I refuse to go there right now.

I mean, he could just stop having feelings for me tomorrow.

I know this is my own deep-seated fear rearing its head.

My therapist would say so, at least. But Hunter is not my dad. He's not going to turn into a monster overnight. I tell myself again that I can't compare Hunter to my dad.

I shake off the lingering anxiety and tug on Hunter's hand.

"Let's walk down to the water," I say. A lot of people have the same idea and are walking the beach away from the bonfires because it's so warm tonight.

As we walk, heat leftover from the day radiates up from the sand at the same time the slightest ocean breeze brushes my bare arms. And I'm suddenly, giddy with the promise of summer in the air. When I moved to L.A. it was late August, still warm, but I didn't hang out at the beach much and then school started.

Now, the thought of spending an entire summer in Los Angeles— hanging out with Hunter as much as possible before college starts and spending every spare second at the beach sounds divine. I might even take up surfing. Or at least take a lesson.

Even as I think this, the dread surfaces again. Summer means college is imminent.

We both have been accepted into the USC film school and so I thought our future together in college was set.

But recently, I learned that during a brief period when we were broken up, Miss Flora spoke to Hunter about applying for a Fulbright Scholarship. The scholarship will pay for him to travel to the slums of Mexico for six months to film a documentary on children taking up arms to protect their village from the cartel.

And Hunter got it.

"I haven't decided yet," he said when he first told me the other day.

As much as I wanted to beg him to stay with me, I knew it was a once-in-lifetime opportunity.

"Of course, you have to go," I told him.

"I don't know."

"You'd be a fool not to go," I said.

"Maybe."

"When do you have to decide?"

"A few weeks."

And then it was dropped. However, it has been looming over our relationship ever since. I'm trying not to let it. But it's hard. I keep reminding myself to live for today.

And today means loving Hunter.

We wander down the beach a ways until we find a spot where nobody else is around.

The moon is nearly full and is beaming down on the ocean in front of us, turning everything an ethereal metallic. I stand there facing the water, taking in the wonder of moonlight on the waves turning them to liquid silver.

I lean back on Hunter who has his arms wrapped around me from behind. I only have on jean shorts and a silky camisole but I don't feel cold at all.

I take out my phone and turn on the camera. Hunter sees me and laughs.

"What?"

"Nothing."

"Come on?" I say smiling back at him.

"Nothing. Just take your picture."

I do and then look at the screen. It's a blob of light and dark.

"There are some things that you just have to capture with your mind's eye," he says and winks.

I stare at the sea and then close my eyes trying to memorize the beauty.

Hunter bends and kisses my bare shoulder, sending shivers down my back.

I hug myself tightly.

"Are you cold?" he whispers.

"No," I say. "I'm just soaking it all in."

I close my eyes and rock back into his warmth. He makes me feel safer than I've felt in God knows how long. There were too many years with my father where feeling safe was something I never thought I'd feel again.

Even as little as a year ago, this life I'm living would've seemed unfathomable. A dream. An alternate universe. That's when my mom and I were in full on survival mode trying to anticipate and dodge my father's alcohol-fueled rage and violence.

As much as I wish it would've never happened, the final act that led to the life we have now is when my dad beat my mom so bad she ended up in the hospital and he ended up in prison.

Now my mom is here, too and she's creating a new life for herself. I've never seen her so happy.

Well, she's a little stressed about finding a job since we are living with her best friend Oscar, but other than that, she seems the most relaxed I've seen her in my life.

"Hey," Hunter whispers in my ear. "Where are you?"

I turn in his arms so I'm facing him. "Right here. Sorry, I was just thinking about how lucky I am. How only a year ago my life was so different."

He leans down and kisses me and I melt into his arms.

"Hey, you two," a familiar voice says.

A voice that sounds almost the same as the first, but not quite, chimes in, "Knock that shit off."

We pull back laughing. It's Hunter's best friends, twins Dex and Devin. Dex has his arm around his girlfriend, and my good friend, Coral.

Seeing them makes me smile. They all are carrying red plastic cups full of booze. It reminds me that I haven't grabbed a drink yet.

"Coral, come grab a drink with me," I say as the guys start high-fiving over some basketball game or something they are talking about.

Hunter grabs me around the waist and gives me a long kiss. He breathes into my ear. "I want you, Kennedy Conner."

His deep husky voice sends tremors of desire through me. Sometimes I look at him and can't bear how beautiful he is with his lean muscled and tanned body, black hockey hair and blazing blue eyes. But it's more than that. There is something about him, his smell, his pheromones, God, I don't know, but whatever it is drives me crazy in a way I never thought possible. Me. The girl who was determined to remain a virgin until she got to college now thinks about sex constantly. It's insane.

I draw away without answering. What can I say? He knows how I feel. His wicked grin as I walk away makes that clear.

Coral laughs. "You guys should probably cut out early tonight."

"For sure," I say.

"I know me and Dex are going to. That boy is looking damn fine tonight."

"Oh?" I say.

"Didn't you see that five o-clock shadow he's got going on? He can rub those whiskers all over my body any day."

"Coral!" I say and burst out laughing. But then grow serious. "Do you think it bugs Devin to be around us? Because he's the only solo dude?"

She grows quiet. But then says, "No. I don't think so. He's so sweet. He's really happy for me and Dex. He always says so. And he is really nice about giving us space."

The twins are known for being incredibly close. Wherever one is, you can find the other. But when Dex and Coral started dating it shifted a little.

"He's a good guy," I say.

"I'm going to try to set him up with Jordan. What do you think?"

"Oh, God, yes!" I say. "She's so cute and sweet."

"I know! I think they would be great together. I just haven't figured out how to set it up. He would be mortified if he knew it was a set up."

We are almost to the parking lot where a bunch of our classmates are standing by the closed trunks of their vehicles. When we get close, they will pop the trunks and offer their wares: any alcohol you can imagine. It's quite a lucrative business, I'm told.

I'm thinking about what Coral said.

"Maybe we can just invite a big group to go to pizza at Jack's and then just sort of arrange it that they sit by each other?"

"Good idea."

Right before we get to the parking lot, there is a huge concrete structure that contains the bathrooms and, during the day, a concession stand.

We decide to stop at the bathrooms before we grab drinks.

When I come out of my stall, I pull up short.

There is a girl leaning against the sink. Waiting for me.

Ava Bradley.

## 2

I glare at her.

AVA BASICALLY MADE my life hell from the first day I walked into Pacific High.

BUT THEN IT got much worse. After Josh Master tried to rape me, Ava fabricated a story and manipulated a video tape to defend him.

I'LL NEVER FORGET that day in court with Ava dressed all in white and me all in black and the judge calling the attorneys into his chambers. The district attorney had leaned over and explained it to me briefly:

"THERE IS SOME NEW EVIDENCE," she said. "A video tape. That's what the *new witness is going to testify about. We're going to go view it in chambers."*

If there was *evidence of the attempted rape—which is the only evidence I could think might exist— why was the district attorney frowning? Ava disappeared with them into the back room. After about thirty minutes, a bailiff announced that court was adjourned until that afternoon. I rushed over to Hunter and my mom and Oscar.*

*"What do you think's going on?" I said, my voice shaking.*

Hunter lifted his phone. *"I've been asking around," he said. "It's not good."*

"Let's go talk somewhere privately," *Oscar said. "I know a place."*

We piled *into the Hummer and went to a coffee shop a few blocks away. It's only when we were seated that Hunter said. "From what I heard Ava has been bragging that she has video footage of that night showing it was consensual."*

I scoffed. "That's impossible." *But I also remembered standing at the bonfire and having her point her camera at me. And the red filming light was on.*

"What do *you think that could mean?" My mom asked Oscar.*

"It depends. *I mean this is where the judge decides whether there's enough evidence to hold Josh over for trial on the charges," he said.*

. . .

UNFORTUNATELY, *the evidence isn't that great. It's basically my word against Josh's. Even though I went to the hospital with scratches on my face, there was no physical evidence of sexual assault.*

AND HUNTER'S *testimony was considered iffy anyway, the district attorney said, because Hunter had beat the shit out of Josh so badly. Josh had a broken nose, black eye and broken ribs. It would not go over well in court even if he explained he had been saving me from Josh.*

I'M WORRIED.

WHEN WE HEADED BACK *to court I soon found out I was right to be worried.*

WHEN WE WALKED IN, *the district attorney was waiting.*

"I'M SO SORRY," *she said.* "The judge dismissed the charges."

"HOW IS THAT EVEN POSSIBLE," *Hunter said, his voice raised.*

SHE BROUGHT *us to her office to explain. Ava had footage of me and Josh kissing and me smiling at him and then she had additional footage of us out by the water with him kissing me. It ended before it showed me trying to get away or throwing me on the ground.*

AND THEN SHE *had extended footage of Hunter beating the shit out of Josh while I sat on the sand and watched. It looked like I had a smile on my face, but it was dark. There was no way I would be smiling.*

"I'M sure you were crying, not smiling, but the light is so bad it's hard to tell," the district attorney said.

*OH, my God.*

BEFORE WE LEFT, *the district attorney took me aside.*

"WHEN WE MET *for the first time you told me that making Josh serve jail time for what he did was less important than making sure other people knew what he was capable of, right?" she asked.*

"YES," *I said, feeling like I was going to vomit.*

"NOW THEY KNOW," *she said. "He has an arrest record for sexual assault and was charged with sexual assault. Even though we lost this case, your bravery matters."*

IT DIDN'T FEEL *that way, though.*

IT FELT *like a punch to the gut.*

HUNTER WAS SO mad I thought he would never speak to Ava again.

·   ·   ·

BUT THEN ONE day Hunter saw his mom on the streets in Hollywood. She'd become a drug addict when he was young and abandoned her family.

SEEING HER AGAIN, sent him spiraling into an alcohol and drug-fueled self-destructive depression. During that crazy time, he sought out Ava's drug dealer and got high with her one night. Well, with her and a group of people including the boy she was dating at the time. But still.

SEEING her now brings back all those awful memories.

"LISTEN, BITCH," she says. "I still owe you for all the fucked-up things you've done to me."

"YOU'RE JOKING, RIGHT?" I actually laugh. "You mean how you lied in court? How you got my boyfriend high? How you've been a manipulative nightmare every second since I met you?"

SHE CROSSES her arms and gives me a snotty smile. "Hunter was my boyfriend first and believe me, he loved getting high with me. Fucking loved it. A whole lot more than he loves staying sober with you."

"FUCK YOU." I react before I realize it. I hate that her words hit home and sting. I know they aren't true, but it still hurts.

THEN SHE'S in my face, a few inches away and I can smell the alcohol on her breath and the sickening cloying perfume. "It's taking every-thing I have not to kick your ass right now," she says.

I LEAN CLOSER AND SAY, "Bring it on, bitch."

JUST THEN A DOOR to the bathroom stall slams open and Coral steps out, black eyes flashing.

"YEAH, BRING IT ON!" she says and makes a show of rolling back her shoulders. I hide a smile. She's such a badass.

AVA'S EYES NARROW. She looks at me and then Coral and back again. Then she steps back.

"THIS ISN'T OVER, yet, New Girl."

"DAMN RIGHT, IT'S NOT," I say.

AVA FLOUNCES OFF. My heart is racing. I swore I would never get in another fight in my life, but I was ready right then. It scares me. I once lost control. I attacked Hunter's ex-girlfriend after she hit him. She landed in the hospital and I was suspended. It took me seeing a therapist to get over my trauma of losing control and attacking someone like that.

IT ALL STEMS from a deep-seated phobia that I'm violent like my dad.

.   .   .

CORAL KNOWS SOME OF IT. She reaches for me.

"DON'T WORRY, I had your back the entire time. I was just biding my time. Element of surprise, you know?"

I SMILE. "I really need a drink now," I say.

"ME, TOO."

WE STOP at the first vehicle we come to and the guy pops his trunk. I pay for a vodka and orange soda and I buy Coral one, too. I start to walk away and then turn back, remembering.

"OH CRAP. I almost forgot Hunter. I need a lemon lime soda," I say.

"THAT'S RIGHT, bad boy doesn't drink anymore, does he?" The voice makes me instantly recoil.

IT'S JOSH MASTERS.

AND SUDDENLY I'M back to that awful night on the beach.

*I'M WIPING my face and steeling myself to return to the party when I hear a voice behind me. Josh Masters.*

*"Kennedy? Kennedy?" He's so close. I stop and turn. The wind has*

*blown my hair in front of my face where it is sticking to my face where my tears were. I push it back and blink.*

*Josh is standing there before me. He takes me in with a long look and then smiles at what he sees.*

*"You are something else."*

*His words are obviously meant to be a compliment, but for some reason they feel like a threat. He steps closer. I step back. He takes another step, and I retreat again, feeling the waves lap at my heel.*

*Before I can move again, he has grabbed my head and pulled me close to him, pressing his mouth to mine. I struggle to get away, but his other arm has looped around my back in a vice-like grip. He is trying to force his tongue into my mouth, and I'm fighting with everything I have. He draws back with his fingers entwined in my hair. I'm pretty sure he's ripping some of it out as he holds me.*

*"Why are you fighting?" he says. "All I want is some of what you gave to Hunter. I promise you'll like it. It will be much better than what he gave you."*

*"Fuck you." I manage to spit the words out around his tongue.*

*He angrily kisses me again, and I bite his lip. Before I can react, he has whirled and thrown me onto the sand, landing on top of me. It knocks the wind out of me.*

*I'm struggling to breathe. His wet mouth is on my neck, and his hands are fumbling under the hem of my dress.*

*I can't get air in. I kick with all my might, but he's too strong. He has pinned me with his forearm over my neck, and I'm starting to worry I'm going to pass out or die if I don't get air quickly.*

*At the same time, I distantly register the sound of him unzipping his pants.*

*I'm starting to see black when I hear a roar and Josh is ripped off me. I gasp for air, staring up at the black night full of stars. There is the sound of scuffling and grunting off to the side, but I'm just trying to focus again. I pull myself up in time to see Hunter get punched in the jaw. He reels back. And then Josh is coming at him, pummeling away. I start to scream.*

. . .

SEEING him here on this same beach is like a slap on the face. And then I notice that Ava is beside him.

I FEEL sick to my stomach.

AVA GIVES ME A NASTY SMILE. "I was just telling New Girl in the bathroom how Hunter sure liked his alcohol when he was with me. He liked lots of things with me."

"SHUT UP, AVA," Josh says and his face darkens.

JOSH IS COMING CLOSER. I start to back up.

CORAL, not usually one to back down, says in a low voice. "Come on, let's go. They're not worth it."

I'VE NEVER SEEN her walk away from a confrontation before. But I follow numbly. I'm shaking madly and furious at my body's reaction to seeing Josh. The last time I saw him had been in court and his stare had nearly sent me running out of the courtroom.

WHEN HE WAS ARRESTED for attacking me, he was kicked off the football team and then kicked out of school. I know that some players on the football team are still mad about it. They blame me. They think he's innocent and that I lied. Thanks to Ava's bullshit manufactured video.

.   .   .

"WHERE YOU GOING? To bring your boyfriend his juice? Need a sippy cup?" he said.

AS SOON AS he insults Hunter, though, my fear evaporates, replaced by protective anger.

"FUCK OFF, JOSH."

WE WALK AWAY, but I'm fuming.

"LET IT GO, KENNEDY," Coral says.

"I HATE HIM."

"I KNOW," she says. "It's just that if we get involved then Hunter and Dex will go nuts and then it will get really ugly."

I SWALLOW MY RAGE. She's right.

WHEN WE GET DOWN to the bonfire, a breeze has kicked up and the temperature had dropped, so now more people are gathered around the fire for its warmth and light. I hand Hunter his drink. He slings his arm around me and suddenly everything is okay again.

I FOLD myself into his embrace.

·  ·  ·

ONE OF HUNTER'S friends from school, Caleb, is telling a funny story about running from cops who were trying to cite them for skateboarding drunk on the Venice boardwalk and everyone is listening and giggling when Josh walks up.

HE'S with two huge football players. Ava is nowhere to be seen.

IN THE FEW weeks since the charges were dismissed, I've mainly avoided running into any football players at school thanks to Hunter. After court, he grew extremely protective of me and walks me to class every day.

I ABSOLUTELY HATE the fact that he feels the need to protect me. But at the same time, I'm not ready for a confrontation again. I've taken self-defense. Some good that did me when Josh attacked me on the beach. And I doubt there's much I could do alone against a bunch of bully football players. So, for now, I won't turn down Hunter's offer to walk me to my classes.

BECAUSE I KNOW AS SOON as it stops, they will pounce. They almost did last week.

HUNTER HAD GONE to the bathroom. I was waiting by my locker. A group of them were standing in the hall staring at me and shooting dirty looks and saying things I couldn't make out.

THE SHEER HATRED pouring off of them was intimidating. But then it got worse. One of them broke away from the group and started walking my way. Before he'd taken more than a few steps, another guy reached out his arm to stop him, pointing down the hall. I looked and saw Hunter heading my way. His smile faded when he took in what was going on.

HE SHOT a glance from the football players to me and then back to them again. He scowled and started to walk past me toward them when I reached out.

"IT'S NOTHING."

HE STOPPED but didn't take his eyes off them.

"YOU SURE?"

"YES," I said. "Let's go."

NOW, on the beach, I recognize the two guys with Josh. One is the football player who had been heading my way. His eyes are narrowed as he watches me and Hunter.

HUNTER SWEARS. "Big fucking mistake coming here," he mutters in a low voice.

MY STOMACH INSTANTLY KNOTS UP.

CORAL, standing with Dex, shoots me a worried look.

.  .  .

"MAYBE WE SHOULD GO," I say, reaching for Hunter's hand.

BUT IT'S TOO LATE.

EVERYONE HAS GROWN quiet as Josh makes his way up to the bonfire and stands across from us. He plants his feet in the sand and stares. A nasty smirk curls his lip up on one side.

NOBODY IS TALKING and you can feel the tension in the air like it's a living thing.

"GOT A FUCKING PROBLEM?" Hunter says, and I know it's begun.

"YOUR GIRL IS MY PROBLEM," Josh says.

I REACH for Hunter's arm. "Don't," I say in a whisper.

I FEEL him tense beneath my touch.

"LET'S JUST GO," I say.

CORAL IS ALREADY LEADING Dex away from the fire toward the parking lot. He stops a few feet away, though and turns, crossing his arms, watching. He won't leave Hunter alone until he knows everything's okay.

.  .  .

DEVIN IS SUDDENLY at Hunter's side. "Let's go, man. He's not worth it," he says loudly enough for everyone to hear.

JOSH CHEWS on his lip and his eyes narrow.

EVERYONE IS WAITING.

IT'S NOT like Hunter to back down. And everyone knows it.

HE SPITS on the ground and turns away. I turn with him, gripping his upper arm.

BUT JOSH ISN'T DONE and starts to speak. Hunter stops. I can feel his body grow tense at Josh's words.

"THAT'S RIGHT, TOUGH GUY," Josh says. "Leave the party to the real men. The ones who can handle their alcohol and don't have to drink their fucking sippy cup juice box."

HE LAUGHS and his stupid football friends join him.

HUNTER PAUSES. I can almost feel the internal struggle in him.

I TAKE a step and tug on his hand.

.   .   .

HE WON'T MEET my eyes. "Hunter?"

STILL HE IGNORES ME.

"HUNTER? Let it go. You're going to blow everything. If you get arrested, they might take retract the Fulbright offer. Please just walk away."

THEN IT'S like I come in focus again and he nods and takes a step.

RELIEF FILLS ME.

AS WE GET FURTHER AWAY, people around the bonfire start talking again and everything seems back to normal.

DEX AND DEVIN and Coral are waiting for us in the parking lot.

HUNTER WALKS up and kicks the tire of his Jeep with his boot. Hard.

"IT'S OKAY, MAN," Devin says. "He's a punk ass douche."

"I WANT TO FUCKING KILL HIM," Hunter says.

DEX IS right by his side. "Me, too, man, me too."

. . .

CORAL IS THERE. "Let's go to my place. I just texted my mom. Her and my dad are in Santa Barbara this weekend, but she says we can totally crash at my house. As long as the guys sleep in the living room and me and Kennedy in my room."

DEVIN LAUGHS. "SHE REALLY TRUSTS YOU?"

"DAMN RIGHT," Coral says. "I do what my mama says. That woman deserves it. I'm not going to disrespect her house."

I LOOP my arm around Coral and hug her. "You're one class act, girl."

"DON'T I KNOW IT," she says and we all laugh.

I TURN TO HUNTER. "Can you live with the rules for a sleepover at Coral's?"

"NO FUCKING WAY," he says.

I LAUGH. "Me, either. But I'm going to."

"SHOULD I INVITE PAIGE AND EMMA?" Coral says, holding her phone.

"TOTALLY," I say. I love spending time with Hunter. But sometimes I miss the days when it was just me, Coral, Paige, and Emma. My squad.

. . .

"PAIGE WAS STUDYING WHEN I LEFT," Hunter offers.

PAIGE IS HUNTER'S STEPSISTER. She says she's already in bed. And Emma says she's babysitting her younger cousins. I'm bummed. It seems that girl time happens less and less.

PAIGE IS ALWAYS super busy lately. She has an internship that is preparing her to go to Stanford in the fall. I hate to think about her leaving. I'm going to miss her so much. While I'm super excited to graduate, and start college, I will miss my friends so much. Even the ones who stay in town will probably be busier so it's all going to be different. You'd think we'd been friends my entire life, not just this school year.

AND THEN THERE IS HUNTER. I refuse to go there right now. I just can't.

I'VE NEVER BEEN to Coral's house so I'm excited. I know it's inland some ways—in Beverly Hills. I don't really know the area. I just know that Coral goes to Pacific High because she had a bad experience at the L.A. arts school.

HER FAMILY USED to live in Pacific Beach, but then moved to Beverly Hills when she was a freshman. She applied and was accepted to the arts school and loved it for the first semester.

UNTIL A SCULPTOR TEACHER fell in love with her. He was thirty years old and married.

. . .

THEY'D GROWN close after school hours when she stayed to learn some advanced techniques. She respected and admired him. They shared laughter and stories and a love of good art. He was a renowned sculpture with his pieces in museums around the world.

BUT THEN ONE DAY, when they were in the studio alone, he tried to kiss her. She didn't let him. She said she was flattered and confused. She'd had a massive crush on him, but didn't know he could tell. So, she also felt super guilty, as if she'd accidentally led him on. Especially when he told her that he wanted to leave his wife. He wanted Coral to move in with him in an apartment in downtown L.A.

CORAL WENT HOME and told her mom. The fallout involved the teacher quitting and Coral going back to Pacific High.

BECAUSE SHE LIVED the furthest away, we never hung out at her house. Until tonight.

ON THE DRIVE OVER, I text my mom and tell her I'm staying over at Coral's.

"THANKS, honey. I'm just finishing up having a glass of wine with our new neighbor Samantha."

I SEND her back a heart emoji. "Have fun."

. . .

I'M SO glad my mom has a friend out here. She's only been living out here a little over a month. She had such big plans, but finding a job has been tougher than she expected. She says it's because she took so much time off work to be a stay-at-home mom. She doesn't say it to make me feel guilty. But I do hope she finds a job soon. Not that we need the money. I mean, we need money, but Oscar pays for everything if we like it or not.

AND HE SAYS we can stay with him as long as we want—at least through my graduation in a few months—but I know my mom is eager to get out and start her new life.

# 3

Hunter is driving his Jeep and we follow behind Coral's car. We take a road that winds up the hills giving really cool views of the city at night.

It takes my breath away to see Los Angeles as night. It's not New York City, but it has its own magic and charm. One thing I know for sure is I'm a city girl. Seeing a skyline just fills me with hope and excitement. For not good reason.

Near the top of the hill, we turn toward a gated community. The gate swings open and we drive even more until there is a giant white house with pillars out front. We all park in the circular driveway.

As we walk up to the porch, the door swings open. A man in slippers and a bathrobe over what looks like silk pajamas smiles. He has gray hair slicked back and a wrinkled face. I wonder if it's her grandfather until he speaks.

"Good evening, Miss Coral," he says.

We step into a foyer with what must be a sixty-foot ceiling. A large staircase looms in front of us that could fit four people across. There are funky black and red ceramic sculptures on top of white pillars scattered throughout the foyer.

"Welcome to Tara," I whisper to Hunter who just nods.

"Hi Hank," Coral says. "These are my friends. They're sleeping over."

"Excellent," he says. "Your mother gave me a heads up and I've set up the hideaway beds in the living room for the young men. I also have set out some snacks if you get hungry."

"Aw, you're the best," Coral says patting his arm as we pass. "We're going to be out at the pool and might be loud. I'll try to keep the music down but if we get too loud, please text me. I don't want to keep you up."

"I will put in my earplugs, then. Thank you for the warning."

And then he is gone and Coral is leading us through the house to the back. I cast a quick look around the rooms as we pass. Everything is super modern with sleek lines and monochrome colors. The back of the house is almost entirely glass overlooking the pool, but as we get to the door, I see the house is shaped in a massive U surrounding the pool.

"Hank?" I say. "Who is Hank?"

She laughs. "He's ... oh, how would I describe Hank?" she says. "He keeps everything running around here. He's been part of our family since my mom was a kid."

"Oh." I have no other words.

Hunter has a live-in maid, but Coral has a manservant. That's the only word I can think of to describe him.

As I follow her past what looks like expensive furniture and paintings, I think about the small Brooklyn apartment I grew up in. We didn't starve and I don't really remember ever wanting for anything, but that's partly because my closest friends, Sherie, and my boyfriend, Ryan, were the same. We all lived in the same area.

We all got jobs at sixteen at fast food places so we had money to go to the movies and subway fare. Thinking of Ryan, I wonder vaguely how he is doing. Our break up was not ideal. He came out here only to discover I was madly in love with Hunter. And Sherie and I had grown apart. We talk about once a month, but she's busy with a new boyfriend and job and so am I. It makes me sad.

Sometimes when I think about my new life, how my closest

friends live in houses like this in Beverly Hills, it doesn't even seem real. Life is so strange sometimes.

We trail Coral into the backyard. The sleek pool has a huge naked woman fountain on one end spouting water out of her mouth like we're in Italy or something. A hot tub is situated at the other end near an outdoor bar.

"There should be swim trunks in the pool house. Kennedy, come with me," Coral says and then leads me off to one side of the pool and opens a door at the very end. It's her bedroom. She has a super big puffy Princess-and-the-pea looking bed with all white sheets and a window seat and huge bathroom with the largest walk-in shower I've ever seen. It has a full on built in bench the size of a love seat.

In her bedroom, she opens the top drawer of a large dresser. "Bikinis in here," she says, plucks one out and heads to another door. "Use my bathroom to change if you want. I'll use one down the hall."

I'm relieved. Despite most people in my gym class being comfortable walking around bare ass naked, I'm not quite that comfortable. I know it's silly, but I appreciate the privacy.

I grab a navy-blue bikini out of her drawer and quickly head to the bathroom. Her bathroom floor is heated and the toilet seat has a heater and revolving neon lights up the bowl.

She's already dressed in a yellow bikini when I step into the bedroom.

Outside, the guys are already doing cannonballs into the pool or trying to throw each other in. Coral steps over to an outdoor bar and flicks on some music. A new song from a rapper I love comes out of speakers. She opens a small refrigerator and grabs a beer for everyone setting them on the bar but then at the last minute I see her return one. Her face crinkles.

Then she opens the refrigerator again and rummages around until she finds a soda.

She pops the tops and then hands each one of us a drink, giving Hunter the soda.

We all pile in the hot tub.

"Oh, my God," I say sinking beneath the hot water, clutching an icy beer above the foaming suds. "This is the life."

For a while we talk about graduation plans. Coral's parents are throwing her a party to beat all parties. "They're trying to get a space at the Getty Museum."

"Can you even do that?" I ask.

She shrugs and tilts the beer bottle up to her mouth.

Hunter clears his throat. "Yeah, I guess some famous director did, once," Hunter says. "I can't remember who it was, Scorsese or Lucas or something, but my dad went. I was too young to go."

"Let's play a game," Coral says. I can tell she's trying to change the subject. For the first time, I realize that her parent's extreme wealth and connections make her uncomfortable.

Everyone sighs and she laughs loudly.

"Spin the bottle?" Hunter asks.

I roll my eyes.

"Truth or dare!" Devin says. I look at him and wonder for the first time if he ever feels like a third wheel around us. He's so sweet. I smile at him.

"No!" Coral says. "Fuck, Marry, Kill."

"Oh no," Dex says. "I can tell this one's going to get me in trouble."

Coral playfully smacks his arm.

"Who wants to go first?" Coral asks.

Hunter groans and throws back his head. "I hate this game."

"Too bad," I say.

"Fine. I'll go. Get it over with."

"You're on, big boy," I say.

Coral looks at him and frowns, thinking.

"Ariana Grande. Miss Cassidy. J-Lo."

"Jesus," he says.

Miss Cassidy is the guidance counselor at school.

"Come on!" I say, laughing. "Spill it. This is a fast game."

He leans back staring at the sky above us. There must be stars up there somewhere, but the smog and lights of L.A. have turned the sky into a hazy orange glow.

"Fuck – J.Lo. Marry? Ariana. Kills? Easy. Miss Cassidy."

"Oh, my God. You would kill poor Miss Cassidy!" Dex says and stands up, pretending to be outraged.

"That's why I hate this game," Hunter says. "No matter what you say, you can't win."

"That's why it's so much fun," Coral says.

Dex goes next. He has to choose between Coral. Her mom. And a cute girl in her twenties who works behind the counter at Jack's Pizza.

"Coral!" he complains. "Are you looking for a reason to dump me? Why? Why would you give me these choices?"

"Just play," she says, laughing.

"Fuck? The pizza girl. Marry? You." Then he stops.

"You'd kill my mom? You'd kill my mom" Coral bursts out laughing. "You sociopath!"

"Hey!" he says. "If I married or fucked her, then you'd kill me."

"True," she says.

When it's my turn, I rub my hands together. "Bring it on."

My choices are Mr. Henry (the chem teacher). Clint Eastwood. And a freshman who just won the national spelling bee.

"Easy," I say. "Marry the smart kid. Fuck Clint. I mean he probably can't even get it up anymore anyway. And kill Mr. Henry. Because his tests are way too hard and everyone would make me the school hero."

"Oh. My. God." Dex says. "If anyone could hear us tonight they'd think they caught a missing clip out of Natural Born Killers."

Hunter and I high five each other. "That's right."

"Okay, Devin," Coral says. "Best for last. Here's your three: Me, Hunter, Dex."

"Fuck you!" Devin says.

"Okay," Coral says. "But who would you marry and kill?"

We all burst into laughter.

We alternate jumping from the pool to the hot tub and back again until it's late and I catch myself yawning.

Devin is snoring on another chair. Dex and Coral are in the hot tub with their heads close together.

Hunter and I are on this loveseat-sized lounge chair that is slightly reclined. We have a blanket on us and are scrolling through our phones.

I'm posting pictures of us on Instagram when Hunter puts down his phone and leans over, putting his head on my shoulder.

I take a selfie of us and then post it. "Look how cute we are," I say. "We look good together."

"Boots, I told you that from day one. It just took you a while to believe me."

"Here, see." I hand him the phone and he is smiling and then suddenly his smile disappears and he thrusts the phone back at me.

"What the fuck, Kennedy?"

I take the phone. There's a notification that disappears as soon as I grab the phone. But I see it for half a second.

DylanRoxy. Dylan is the lead singer in a boy band, Sunset Patrol.

I'd met him at a Hollywood club. And for whatever, reason he hasn't stopped pursuing me, saying he respects my relationship with Hunter but that he's waiting for it to end, basically. We kissed once or twice but only when Hunter and I were briefly broken up a few months ago when he was using and drinking. Dylan is super sweet. But he's not Hunter.

But all Hunter sees is a threat.

*Hunter thrusts his phone out at me. "This."*

*I blink. "What?"*

*It's a TikTok. I look at the username. Sunset Patrol. My heart sinks.*

*"It's not what you think."*

*"Just watch it and then tell me what you think I think," Hunter says in a nasty tone.*

*I hit play. It's Dylan kissing my palm and then it cuts to him kissing my cheek. The words on the TikTok say, "When you meet the girl of your dreams but have to catch an early morning flight."*

*"I had no idea someone was filming," I say without thinking.*

*I'm slightly horrified, but also flattered. Because its TikTok it plays on repeat. I wince. I'm sure it is horrible for Hunter to see.*

*Hunter draws back, eyes wide as if I've punched him. "That's all you have to say about it?"*

*I reach for his hand. "No. It's nothing. I swear," I say. He jerks his hand out of mine. He backs away from me.*

*"Hunter, you're drunk so I'd rather talk about this tomorrow, but I swear what you see is what you get." Again, wrong thing to say.*

*"Jesus fucking Christ, what are you trying to say, Kennedy?" He sounds so hurt my heart is breaking.*

*I exhale loudly. "We sat with his band. That's it. We told all of them we had boyfriends right off the bat. It was purely platonic."*

*He closes his eyes as if he's using the last shred of patience. Then his eyes fly open. "Why is he fucking kissing you, then?"*

*I frown. "I don't know. I told him it was inappropriate. He's just sort of an affectionate person. Honestly, Hunter it means nothing. I swear. I'm never going to see him again."*

*He sees my phone clutched in my hand at my side and looks at it pointedly.*

*"He's just sort of an affectionate person?" he repeats. "You fucking know him that well?"*

*I wince again. "Hunter—" I begin, but don't know what to say.*

*"So, you didn't arrange to stay in touch? Like you don't have his phone number or Snap?"*

*I can feel my face grow hot.*

*"It was his idea."*

*"Of course, it was." He strides by me angrily toward the front door.*

*"Hunter?"*

*"I'm outta here."*

Now, I put the phone down on the table next to me face down. I haven't heard from Dylan for months. And so of course he Snaps me right when Hunter is holding my phone. Fuck.

"Aren't you going to check the Snap and see what he sent?" Hunter asks, raising an eyebrow and sitting up so he's higher than me.

I sit up, too.

"No," I say.

"Why not?"

"Because you're my boyfriend."

"That doesn't mean you can't check a Snap message from another guy."

I turn to him. "You're right. I know we don't have that kind of relationship."

"So, check it."

I'm wary. I've been trying to play it cool, but I don't like this game he's playing.

"What the fuck, Hunter? You a glutton for punishment?"

"Whatever. I'll be gone in a few months anyway and then you can do whatever the hell you want."

I reel back. It's like a punch to the gut.

He sees my face. "I didn't mean that, Boots."

He's standing and before I can react, he takes a few long strides and dives into the pool. He swims a few laps. I sit on the edge of the chair watching, full of hurt and anger. I've encourage him to accept the Fulbright Scholarship and go to Mexico, even though it will break my heart and then he throws it back on me like a slap in the face.

Finally, he pulls himself out of the pool and grabs a towel. He dries himself as he walks and then wipes off his face and hair as he gets to me. He hovers over me, water dripping on the ground.

"I didn't mean that," he says looking down on me.

"Cooled off, now?" I ask in an icy tone.

He sits down beside me, so close that our thighs are touching and my flesh erupts into goosebumps. "Listen. I don't want to be a jealous boyfriend."

"Good," I say. "Because I don't want to be a jealous girlfriend."

He smiles at me. "You're not. You're great."

"You're great, too." I say and smile back.

"Barf," I hear a voice say and look up to see Devin getting up from the lounge chair near us. "I'm going to bed before I choke on my own vomit listening to you two."

We laugh, but don't speak again until he heads inside.

I pick up my phone and thrust it at Hunter. "Here, you check it. I haven't heard from him in months. Last time we talked I reminded him that I have a boyfriend."

My hand is holding out the phone and suddenly I realize how stupid this move was. I haven't done anything wrong but what if Dylan is professing his undying devotion to me and Hunter reads it? That would suck for Hunter.

Luckily, he doesn't take my phone. He shakes his head.

"I trust you."

"Good," I say.

"I don't need to see it."

"Okay."

"Aren't you going to check it or respond?" he says.

I shake my head. "No."

"Why?"

"Because even if you aren't jealous and say it's okay, I don't want to do anything that could be misconstrued or that might hurt your feelings. Even if you weren't sitting right there with me."

"Thanks."

"No problem." I yawn.

"You should go to bed."

We look at Coral and Dex. She is kissing him at the door to the living room. Then Dex goes inside and Coral walks over to her bedroom door. She walks in, leaving the door open for me.

I lean over and kiss Hunter a long goodbye. He walks me to the door to Coral's bedroom and gives me another kiss. He pulls back, groaning.

"Whose idea was this for a segregated sleepover?" he grumbles.

"You'll live," I say.

But I stay pressed up against him. He looks down at me and smiles. "But will you?"

He knows me so well. He knows my body is on fire for him.

"Barely," I whisper.

Then I hear Coral. "Keep it down out there."

"Uh oh," I say into the open door. "Are you the crabby type when you're tired?"

"You have no idea," she says.

"Fuck."

"Just don't wake me in the morning or there'll be hell to pay. You guys help yourself to anything but don't wake me, no matter what."

"I think she's serious," I say in a mock whisper.

Hunter and I laugh. "Good to know," he says.

In Coral's room, she hits a button and a Murphy bed folds down from the wall.

"Cool," I say. But she's already in bed with her eye mask on and it sounds like she's asleep by her deep breathing.

# 4

I'm deep into some dark dream involving blood and broken dishes at my old house in Brooklyn when I'm woken by someone shaking my shoulder.

"Kennedy?" someone whispers. It's either Dex or Devin but in the dark, I can't tell.

"What?" I sit up. There is some light streaming in from the open door to the hall. I'm confused.

"It's Hunter," he whispers. I can tell now it's Devin.

I'm up with my phone in my hand following him out of the room. He leads me down the hall to the living room. The lights are on and Dex is sitting on one of the massive couches with his phone to his ear. Hunter is nowhere to be seen.

"Answer, man!" Dex says.

Alarm zings through me.

"What's going on?"

"Hunter got a text from his dad," Dex says.

"Oh no." I immediately think of my friend, Hunter's stepsister. "Is Paige okay?"

Very few people in our friend group know that she was pregnant a few months ago and miscarried. It was a wake-up call for her. She broke up with her college boyfriend, got an internship and spends every waking minute working on school and prepping for her intensive courses at Stanford in the fall. She's probably the smartest one of any of us with the most potential for her future.

It had broken my heart when she got pregnant and was talking about trying to go to college with a baby. If anyone could've done it, she could've, but I was so happy she didn't have to figure out how to make that work.

Dex answers my question.

"Paige is fine. It's Hunter's mother."

My heart sinks.

"What about his mom?"

His mother is a recovering addict. She's only been out of detox for a few weeks now. Hunter's parents are divorced but his dad set her up in a little apartment in Long Beach and helped get her a job waiting tables. I met her once. She was really nice.

I know Hunter's still dealing with growing up with a mother who was an addict. She basically abandoned her family when he was young. He only recently forgave her when they were both in detox together. I worry that she's relapsed. I know that is going to be really tough for him to hear. They are only now forming a new relationship. He will be so disappointed.

Nobody has responded, so I ask again.

"What about his mom?"

Dex turns to me.

"She overdosed."

## 5

Finally, Hunter returns Dex's texts and calls.

He only types three words, "Long Beach Memorial."

I jump up. "Let's go."

They are already on their feet, as well.

Devin and Dex say I can ride with them to the hospital.

"Is Coral okay with us leaving her?" I ask.

He nods. "Don't wake her up. That girl needs her sleep. She can come when she wakes up. We'll know more then."

"If she's mad I'm blaming you," I say.

"She'll be mad if we wake her," Dex says.

We leave a note for Coral and head out in Devin's SUV.

It takes thirty minutes for us to get to the hospital. When we first leave, I send Hunter a text just saying we are on our way.

He doesn't respond.

The freeway is surprisingly crowded for the middle of the night. I am sick to my stomach with worry about Hunter's mom, Elizabeth. I'm so worried she's going to die. That would be tragic, of course, but I worry about what it will do to Hunter. He really only just got her back as a mom.

At the hospital, we park and then find the emergency room. Hunter isn't there.

Devin speaks to someone at the information desk and we are told that Mrs. West has been admitted to the hospital in intensive care. They give us her room number and we take the elevator up.

Hunter is in a small waiting room. There is another family with red eyes, as if they have been crying. They are huddled in a corner. Hunter is sitting on the edge of a chair, his hands over his knees, his boots tapping. He looks up when we file in.

When I see the look on his face I want to run over and hug him. He looks devastated. I'm scared to death suddenly that she is dead.

Somehow Dex beats me to Hunter who stands and they hug.

Then Hunter turns to me and Devin. Devin slaps his shoulder. "You okay, man?"

He shakes his head. "It's fucked up."

I reach for him and he grabs me and hugs me tightly, his chin resting on my shoulder and his face buried in my hair. I hug him hard. I don't know what to say.

We all sit down then.

"Where's your dad, man?" Devin asks.

"He's in with her. They are letting us see her one at a time."

I'm terrified to ask anything so I just reach for his hand.

He exhales loudly and then starts to talk, running his hand through his hair.

"They found her in an alley down by the aquarium," he says. "They think she got a bad dose of something. It's going around. They had to give her Narcan, which should've revived her, but it didn't do what it was supposed to. The person who called 911 said she was having a seizure and then stopped breathing. They are worried that she stopped breathing too long and may have some brain damage."

His voice chokes on the last few words.

"Oh, no," I say.

Just then Hunter's dad comes out. He's wearing designer jeans and a baseball cap pulled low. I can't really see his face.

He glances at us and pats Hunter's shoulder. "You can go in, now, son."

Hunter stands, releasing my hand.

My heart is breaking as I watch him walk toward the door.

Mr. West watches as well until Hunter is gone. Only then does he turn to all of us.

"Thank you for coming," he says. I notice he doesn't meet my eyes. His eyes glance over me and focus on the twins.

"Hunter is lucky to have friends like you."

Friends. I bristle at the term. I've been with Hunter for more than six months, but Mr. West acts like I'm some fly-by-night girl. I realize I resent the fuck out of that and also realize that he obviously doesn't approve of me for his son. It sucks.

I flinch remembering when he looked at me in a bikini and made me feel unattractive and unworthy of Hunter's attentions.

Devin reaches out to me and pats my knee. I smile at him gratefully.

"Hunter's lucky to have a girlfriend like Kennedy," he says. "Someone he can really count on." I smile at him gratefully.

Mr. West doesn't even fucking answer. He reaches for his phone. It looks like he's texting someone.

Then he stands. "Tell Hunter I'll be back in a few hours. I've got to take care of some business."

And then he's gone.

I know that my feelings shouldn't matter right now, but his dismissal of me stings.

"Kennedy, don't worry about Mr. West," Dex says. "He's a little icy when you first get to know him, but he's not really that bad."

I make a face.

"If it makes you feel any better, we had to be friends with Hunter for like ten years before he even acknowledged we existed. It's just how he is," Devin says.

I shake my head and look away. They are trying to cheer me up.

The mint green walls with the ocean scenes are supposed to be soothing, I know, but they are stressing me out. I want to stand and pace, but that would be weird, so I just pick at my nail polish until there are blue flakes everywhere.

My phone dings.

"Bitch, where are you?" It's a text from Coral.

I text her back what's going on and say, "I was afraid you'd murder me if I woke you."

"I'll be there in thirty, though. My Spidey senses picked up that something was wrong so I'm wide awake."

Hunter is still gone when Coral rushes in.

She's wearing a long red skirt to her ankles and a big puffy fur jacket. It's the middle of the night, but she has on dark sunglasses. Nobody can ever say that Coral doesn't know how to make an entrance.

Both Dex and I stand and she runs over and throws her arms around both of us.

When we untangle ourselves, she props her sunglasses on her head and asks where Hunter is.

Before we can answer, I spot Hunter coming down the hall. I'm trying to read his body language. But I can't tell a thing. And his face is expressionless.

"Hey, Coral," he says in a subdued voice.

"How is she?" I ask.

He shakes his head. I stand and hug him.

"Want to go for a walk?" I ask.

He nods.

We head downstairs and then outside.

He leans against the brick wall of the hospital. "She looks so bad, Boots. So, bad."

"I'm so sorry," I say.

He doesn't say anything.

An ambulance pulls in with sirens blaring. We turn and watch as the paramedics unload an elderly man on a gurney. He has tubes coming out of his face.

They rush him inside.

I hate hospitals. Hate them. When I used to be hooked on Grey's

Anatomy, I'd considered becoming a nurse, but now I want all my hospital visits to only be done from the safety of my living room TV.

Hunter reaches for my hand. I squeeze it tight. I don't know what to say. Usually our conversation is so easy and flowing, but this is different. I don't know the right thing to say to help make him feel better. But I need to try, so I ask, "Want to talk about it?"

He shrugs as if he doesn't know, but begins to talk.

"She had all these tubes and stuff and machines and they keep the lights low. It is just really weird. It sucks to see her like that. Don't get me wrong, most years of my life after she disappeared, I expected to next see her in a coffin. But I never really imagined a hospital bed."

"You were in there quite a while," I say.

He looks down at his boots. "I was telling her all the shit I always wanted to tell her. In case."

I squeeze his hand harder.

"I told her a lot of things when we were in Palm Springs together," he says, referring to the time they were both in detox not long ago.

"That's good, Hunter." I smile.

He pulls away from me and begins to pace. "I just can't handle it if she's taken away from me right when I just got her back."

His voice cracks.

"I know," I say.

He stops pacing and stares at me, his blue eyes boring through to my soul. Then he answers, "I know you, do."

In a second, I'm in his arms and he's lifting my chin up and kissing me.

"I don't know what I would do without you, Boots," he says in a low voice.

He pulls back and searches my eyes. "You help me keep my shit together."

"Um, okay." I laugh.

He laughs, too. It's good to hear the sound.

"I mean, my first instinct right now is to go look for something to drink. I mean I want to get fucked up so badly. I feel all this shit and I don't want to feel it I want to drink until I don't feel it anymore."

I exhale loudly and nod. "Yeah. I can see where you'd want to do that."

"But I look in your eyes and I know that's the coward way out," he says.

"I'm proud of you."

It wasn't long ago, I thought he would pick alcohol and drugs over me. And a chance at a normal life.

*I look at my phone to see what time it is—1 a.m.—and see ten missed calls and just as many texts. Hunter. I guess I know who's at the door. I push the door open and turn and walk away. He hurries inside.*

*"I know. I blew it. I was over at Craig's house and he offered me some beer and one thing led to another. And then I had to wait until I was okay to drive. And I came straight here. Can you give me another chance?"*

*I look at him. He looks awful. I don't even know who Craig is. That's how far apart we've become. There are so many things I could say. But instead, I shake my head.*

*"I need some time, Hunter."*

*"How long?"*

*"I don't know," I say honestly. "I told you I can't be with someone I can't count on."*

*"I know that." His voice is quiet. But his eyes are wild. "I'm such a fuck up." He mumbles it under his breath. I don't have the energy to feel bad for him. I'm over it.*

*"Just go, Hunter," I say.*

*I love him. But I love sober Hunter. Drunk Hunter is a whole different story.*

The memory of him drinking and using drugs is still fresh and still stings.

"I want to be a better person for you," he says now.

I've been holding back tears all night but can't do it anymore. I can feel them slipping down my cheeks. He leans over and brushes them away with the pad of his thumbs and then draws me close.

Just then Dex is rushing out the door.

"Hunter? They're asking for you."

Heart pounding, I follow Hunter as we race inside.

In the elevator, Hunter asks, "What did they say?"

Dex shakes his head. "Nothing, man, just asked for you."

Hunter's face is ash white.

I've got a vice-like grip on Hunter's hand and he's squeezing back just as hard. Nobody is talking. I think we're all scared to death.

Finally, the elevator stops and the door whooshes open. Hunter races toward the ICU while Dex and I stand there staring after him.

"Fuck," I say.

"Exactly," Dex says.

After about twenty minutes, Hunter comes back in. We all jump to our feet.

"She's going to be okay."

Coral starts to cry. I think I'm too stunned to cry.

"She woke up," he says. "And she seems normal. I mean, mostly normal."

That's when my tears come. I run over and bury my face in his chest and he leans down and hugs me back.

After a while, Hunter tells us we all should go home.

"I'm going to wait here. My dad is going to be back soon," he says.

"Are you sure?" I ask. I feel guilty but I'm exhausted, asleep on my feet.

He nods. Then he leans over and says, "Thanks for being here," in a choked-up voice.

"Of course."

Coral drops me off at home and I crawl into bed. My mother and Oscar are not on the main floor and I don't check their bedrooms. It's only six in the morning so they might still be sleeping. I'm too tired to explain everything. I just want to sleep.

A FEW HOURS later I wake and smell coffee.

It's nearly ten.

I check my phone. Hunter hasn't texted. I shoot him a text.

"Hope you're sleeping. I'm up if you want to call or message. x."

My mom smiles when she sees me pad into the kitchen. She's sitting at the bar with someone I don't recognize. The woman has huge lips, long reddish hair, and is wearing a short skirt and low-cut top. In other words, she's probably in her forties, but dressed like she's in her twenties.

Her legs are crossed and her thighs are tan and super skinny. Her face doesn't have any wrinkles, but her neck is creased, which Oscar told me is a telltale sign of going under the knife. She looks a little plastic-like. Her features look almost too perfect. She's really pretty, but in a Barbie doll way. She's sort of what I think of as the typical L.A. woman.

She and my mom are both holding steaming mugs of coffee.

I blink and realize it's our neighbor who only recently moved in. I've only seen her out on her deck a few times. She has always struck me as a bit odd and now, when she first looks at me, something odd flashes across her face. It makes me uncomfortable. It's a lot like the look Hunter's dad gives me: an assessment they find lacking in some way or less than.

Her eyes with the huge fake lashes sweep over me from head to toe and then she looks away dismissively. I swallow the insecure feeling this gives me.

But then my mom says, "Kennedy, this is Samantha."

And it's as if her faces shifts. Her eyes are back on me. And I almost wonder if I imagined her earlier disdain, because her face lights up with a big warm smile. She jumps up and hugs me.

"So, nice to meet you, honey," she says. "I've heard so many great things about you."

I smile, but I'm incredibly uncomfortable. I swear half a second before that the look on her face was saying something entirely different.

I squirm out of her grip and turn away. "Hi, mama."

"How was your sleepover?" she asks, smiling brightly. It's great to see her like this, so full of life and not beaten down and downtrodden like she was when she was married to my father. I'm so happy she has a friend, but I'm super fucking suspicious of this woman. I glance at her and she smiles.

"Kennedy?" my mom says again.

"Actually, it was pretty awful. Hunter's mom overdosed."

Samantha gasps and slams down her coffee so it splashes all over the counter. She doesn't even notice. Her eyes are wide and watching me. "Oh, my God."

I give her a look thinking, "What the fuck?" But my mom hasn't noticed.

Instead, my mom is reaching for me. "Oh no. Is she okay?"

"I think so," I say, sneaking a glance at Samantha who seems to have regained her composure. "I was at the hospital most of the night with him."

My mom is hugging me. "I'm so sorry."

"I'll probably go over there this morning."

"Of course."

Meanwhile Samantha looks flustered. She gathers up her purse and a sweater. "I'm sorry, Justine, I have to run. I didn't realize I was late. Let's talk later."

And she's gone.

I stare after her.

"What's up with her?" I say.

My mom smiles. "She's a divorcee, too. I think she's lonely. She seems like she needs a friend."

I press my lips together.

That wasn't what I meant. Why did she act so fucking weird when I mentioned an overdose? Something is off about her. I can't put my finger on it, but I don't like it. My mom is really vulnerable right now.

My mom clears her throat. "I might do some work for her."

"Really?" I say and now I'm really uncomfortable. "You sure that's a good idea?"

My mom shoots me a look.

I scramble to explain. "Um, you know, working for a friend?"

"I'm sure it will be fine. She needs someone to do her books and accounting so it would be a good job for me to gain some experience and a reference. And without a car, it would be super easy since she lives right next door," my mother says brightly.

"Oh," I say. Then pause. "What does she do anyway?"

My mom is clearing the coffee cups now and has her back to me. "Something to do with online sales or something."

Of course. Something nebulous. Just like her.

My phone dings. It's a text from Hunter. "Home. Going to sleep."

I'm about to get up when my mom turns to me. "Don't you like her?"

Instantly I feel guilty. "No, it's fine, mom. I guess I feel a little protective of you."

My mom bursts into laughter. "Kennedy, you don't have to worry about me, honey. You've done enough of that in your life," she says, suddenly growing serious. "It's your turn to take care of yourself. I'm sorry you ever had to feel that way."

I feel tears prick at my eyes so I smile and turn away. "Better go get ready."

All I want to do is go hug Hunter and make sure he's okay. I dress in oversized joggers and a crop top, but throw a black velvet hoodie over it. I slip on my Vans and some lip gloss and perfume and leave.

I drive through the coffee shop on the way and pick up two iced lattes in case he's awake. If he's not, the lattes will last until later since they are iced.

When I get to Hunter's place, all the cars are gone from the driveway except his Jeep. The door to his room above the garage is unlocked. I creep up the stairs, cringing as they creak in case he's asleep. It's so quiet, I think he must be.

When I get to the top of the stairs, the room is dark from his black out curtains but there is a small purple night light that casts the room in a nocturnal glow. I set down the drinks, kick off my shoes and slip into bed beside him, wrapping my arms around him from behind.

He makes a cute mumbling sound and reaches for my hands and then falls back into a deep sleep.

When I wake later, the light has changed and Hunter is still asleep. I sneak out of bed and order a pizza and sodas. I am able to go meet them at the gate and get back in the room without waking him. By now it's five.

I have set up the food and drinks on his desk when I hear him stir in the bed. I look over and he's sitting up with his hair sticking up everywhere. He's adorable.

"Hungry?"

"I thought I was dreaming. Pizza!"

I bring him a paper plate with slices of pizza and a soda. He wolfs down a piece before I even return with my own plate. I shove some napkins at him.

"Don't get sauce on your sheets."

He takes a big slurp of his soda and turns to me. "Is there more?

"Oh yeah."

He gets out of bed and pads over to the desk. He's wearing shorts and nothing else. Seeing his bare back takes my breath away. He's so gorgeous.

He settles back in with four slices stacked.

"Jesus, this is the best pizza I've ever had. Where'd you get it, Jacks?"

"No way," I say and take another bite.

Jacks is the local hang out where everyone at Pacific High gets their pizza.

He squints at me. "Give it up, Boots."

I smile. I love how playful he is. I'm relieved since last night was so scary.

"It took me and Oscar many days of reconnaissance to find this place, I'm not giving you the name for free."

He gets a wicked look in his eyes. Then he leans over and takes my plate out of my hands. "Hey!" I say. He sets it down on the nightstand with his own plate and then crawls on top of me.

"What are you doing? I'm hungry," I say with a laugh.

"Me, too, Boots," he says in a low-throated voice. "Me, too. Very, very hungry."

By the time, he's tugging at my T-shirt to get it over my head, I'm just as frantic to get undressed as he is.

But then just as suddenly, when I am naked beneath him, he slows down. He climbs out of bed.

"Wait here."

"Get back here," I growl at him. I start to pull the blankets over my naked body.

"No!" he grows it and I freeze. "Stay just the way you are."

I laugh. "So bossy."

He doesn't answer. I hear something rattle as if he's taking a sip of our sodas and jiggling the ice.

A few seconds later he's back. I hear him set something down on the nightstand. I start to lift my head to see what it is, but he takes a palm and gently pressed my chest back down to the bed and says, "Ssshhh...."

I start to grumble and he says, "Do you trust me?"

He is leaning over me, his eyes boring into mine. I nod.

Then he lifts the back of my head and slips something around my eyes. Something silky. A blindfold of some sort.

Then I hear the rattle of something in a glass. Before I can figure out what it is, I feel it. He is running an ice cube down my neck, across my clavicle and down between my breasts. I gasp in a swirling mix of pain and pleasure.

I want to squirm away but it feels so good. I don't think I can feel anymore electrified but then his hot mouth is on me tracing the path of the ice cube.

Then his mouth is by my ear again. "Give me the name, Boots. Now."

It takes a few seconds to register what he's talking about. The pizza place.

I burst out laughing. "No way."

"Fine," he says. "Have it your way."

Then his mouth is all over me. Driving me crazy. He's teasing me to the brink and then drawing back his mouth and his hands and his body and I'm starting to get irritated.

"Knock it off," I say. "Get over here now!"

"Tell me you want me," he says.

"I want you in me this instant, Hunter West!" I say, reaching for him. He leans back just out of my grasp.

"Pizza place?"

"You're a monster!" I say.

He is laughing so hard now, he's doubled over.

Then he's on me again. His full weight pressed on me and I can feel how bad he wants me and I'm moaning and going to explode even without him inside me when he pulls back again.

He is holding himself above me.

"Hunter!" I'm starting to get pissed now.

"This is entirely your fault because you're being stubborn," he says. "All you have to do is say the name."

He's right. I'm stubborn as fuck. And I'm going to win this little game. Even if my body is fighting against me every second. I realize I didn't even know what sexual frustration was until this very second. It's awful.

I shake my head.

"Over my dead body," I say.

"Is that how you want to play?" he asks in a low voice.

Then I feel my arms yanked above my head and my wrists cinched together in something silky.

As he cinches the fabric tighter I start to scream and bite and kick and see white.

Hunter instantly unties me and is holding me in his arms. I realize I'm weeping uncontrollably. He's murmuring in my ear, "Oh, my God. I'm so sorry. I'm so sorry."

It even takes me a few seconds to realize why I reacted that way, what triggered me like that.

Carly. She'd handcuffed me to this very bed and stuck a needle in me.

*"Hunter?"*

*Before I get the word out, I'm hit with something that drops me to my knees. I'm reeling in pain, trying to recover, when I feel something cold snap on my wrists. Handcuffs.*

*What the fuck?*

*A small light on the desk flicks on.*

*Carly stands there, chest heaving, panting. A wild look in her eyes.*

*"Where's Hunter? What did you do to him?"*

*"I didn't do anything to him except give him the best sex of his life."*

*"Where is he?" I shriek. I look around and see a crumpled bundle in the corner. I scream. As soon as I do, I'm slapped across the face.*

*"If you don't shut up, I'll gag you."*

*I nod to show I agree.*

*"Get on the bed, you whore," she says.*

*I scramble over to the bed, trying to see whether the dark blob in the corner is Hunter. As I walk past, I see it's not him and am filled with relief. There is another set of handcuffs with one attached to the metal bed frame.*

*"Back up."*

*"Fuck you."*

*She slaps me again. "If you don't do what I say, Hunter is going to die."*

*So, I back up and hear her click the handcuffs together.*

*Then she bursts into giggles.*

*"You're such a dumb bitch," she says. "You think I would hurt Hunter?"*

*I glare at her and don't answer.*

*She walks over to Hunter's desk, and I see she is doing something that involves a needle. My blood runs cold.*

*Whirling, she taps the needle. "Hunter said he'd never date a girl who did drugs," she says. "You know why?"*

*I shake my head.*

*"His mom?" Carly says. "She was an addict. He hates her."*

*Then she smiles. And for some reason I'm filled with insane jealousy that I didn't know this about Hunter and she did. And she knows it.*

*"Guess you don't know him that well after all, do you?" she says and adds, "Or he just doesn't care for you enough to share that."*

*I try to ignore her digs. I need to keep my wits about me and stop her from putting that needle into me. She's clearly fucking nuts so I need to operate with that in mind. Her weak spot is Hunter. Same as my own Achilles' heel.*

*"Did you know that Hunter's mom cheated on his dad?"*

*I stare at her.*

*"Did you know they stayed together as 'best friends' until she turned into a drug addict."*

*She's chatty. I need to distract her, to talk her out of whatever she has planned.*

*Now she is by the side of the bed.*

*"Listen, Carly," I say. "I know that you and Hunter had something special. And I know it's hard for you to see him with me. But if you hurt me he will never forgive you. You know that, don't you?"*

*Instead of answering, she bursts into laughter.*

*And before I can react, she lunges and plunges the needle into my neck. I fight for a few seconds, and then it's game over. She has her knees on my arms, and they are pinning me, digging in and keeping me from moving. But it's more than that. It's whatever she's stuck into my neck. It's taken away my ability to fight or even move. I'm jelly. My arms and legs are too heavy to lift. My head lolls to one side, and it seems like too much effort to turn it forward again. At the same time, an amazing feeling of heat swarms over me.*

*"What was in that needle?" I say. My voice sounds like it is coming from far away.*

*"Something that will make you feel good. And then bad."*

*Then she's gone.*

*I slip into a hazy feeling of warmth and coziness. Frolicking images—of people laughing, the mesmerizing dance of flickering bonfires, and waves crashing —scroll down the movie screen in my mind, even though my eyes are closed. Time kaleidoscopes. I don't know if it's been seconds, hours, or days when Hunter's face appears before me.*

*He seems to hover in the darkness above me.*

*"Oh, my God, Kennedy. What the fuck?"*

Now I pull back from Hunter and push him away, overcome by the memory.

"I can't breathe," I say. "Give me a little room."

He's up and pacing the wooden floors of the bedroom raking at his hair.

"Jesus. Fuck. I'm such an ass. Fuck me. I totally forgot. I'm so sorry, Kennedy, can you ever forgive me?" he says it in a rush as he paces, shooting a glance my way very once in a while.

Once I catch my breath, and realize why I acted that way, I'm over it.

Hunter looks wracked. The look he gives me is heartbreaking. At the same time, my body is still on fire. He brought me to the edge and then left me hanging. Even my freak out didn't diminish my desire to have him in me harder and deeper than he ever has before. The power of this desire is nearly terrifying.

"Hunter?" he keeps pacing.

"Hunter!" I yell this time.

He freezes and turns toward me.

I smile at him.

I can practically see the relief flood through him.

"Kennedy?"

I crook my finger at him. "I can only forgive you if you get your ass over here right now and do exactly as I say."

He does.

# 6

We go to the hospital later that night.

Thank God, his mother, Elizabeth is out of ICU and sitting up in her hospital bed.

She gives us a wan smile when we walk in.

Hunter is so sweet. He leans down and kisses his mom's cheek and I've never loved him more. That woman broke his heart in a million pieces and has given him every reason over the years to despise her and yet his heart is so big that he just loves her unconditionally now.

When he draws back, she reaches out for me. I go to the bed and hold her hands as she speaks.

"It is so nice to see you, Kennedy."

The first time I met her, well really met her (if you don't count when she was high on Hollywood Boulevard that one time), was at the Palm Springs detox where she and Hunter reconciled. She was very sweet to me then and I could see how she was when she was clean and sober. And I know that's what Hunter got to see while he was there, as well.

She clears her throat. "Although it's always wonderful to see you, I must admit, I'm terribly embarrassed that it's under these circumstances. Do you think?" She shoots a glance at Hunter, "after I get out of detox again that you and I can do a girl's lunch or something?"

"I'd like that," I say and smile. And I mean it. "I read that book you were reading at the ... in Palm Springs."

She tilts her head quizzically. "Which one? I'm afraid I was on quite a reading tear while I was there."

I say the title. The one about the inner child and forgiveness.

She claps her hands together. "That is a good one."

"I just wanted to say that it really helped me figure some things out," I say.

"I'm so glad. It helped me figure some things out, too," she says and looks at Hunter.

He blushes.

"Hunter I cannot believe how proud I am of you," she says. "A Fulbright Scholar. Good God, am I impressed. I may not have done very many things right in my life, but having you is the biggest blessing of my life."

He looks down.

"Listen, I'll wait in the hall. I've got to call my mom," I say. "I'm glad you're okay."

It's a lie about calling my mom, but I want them to have some privacy. She smiles but doesn't say anything else and I know it's good that I'm leaving them alone.

Plus, the Fulbright Scholar thing sends me spiraling down to a place I don't want to go. I wonder if he's told her if he's accepted. He hasn't told me anything.

In the hall, I check social media on my phone. It's all pretty boring. I return a few messages from Coral and Paige and Emma, filling them in and telling them I'll see them all at school tomorrow.

"Girls only lunch?" Coral says.

"Totally," I reply.

Hunter will be fine. He has Dex and Devin. They are like brothers.

Hunter comes out and loops his arm around my neck, leaning down to kiss the top of my head.

"Let's get you home before I have to take you back to my room and torture you for the name of that pizza place again."

"Bring it on."

## 7

The next day at school, I kiss Hunter goodbye in the hall after our film class. He dropped because of rehab, but our teacher, Miss Flora, asked him to come back. She really thinks he has talent.

Today, she asked us both to stay after class. After the other students file out she told us she submitted our short romance film to the Santa Barbara Film Festival.

"No way!" Hunter says.

She beams. "It was by far the best one in the class. I think it has some real potential."

"Wow," I say.

We make appointments with her to come in individually during lunch this week so she can film an interview with us.

"They want the teachers to do an interview and then submit an excerpt of the interview with the film."

Hunter and I look at each other. "Okay," we both say.

Out in the hall, the first bell has already rung. We have to hurry or we'll be late for our next class, even though Miss Flora gave us passes.

"You need me to walk you to class?" Hunter asks.

He's walked me every single day since the attack by Josh. It stops me in my tracks that he is questioning doing it again.

He looks down at me. "I can, you know," he says. "But I think you got this on your own, Boots."

It's weird. And flattering. I don't know what to think about it. When I hesitate, he says. "You know, I've been late to second hour every single day. I probably should try to get there on time the rest of the year."

That's why. I laugh. "Go on," I say and push him away. "I'm fine."

He winks. "I know you are."

I watch him walk away as the halls fill with students passing classes. I follow him for some ways until I get to the stairs that lead to my second-floor class. For some reason, I stay at the foot of the stairs and watch him and then something odd happens. He turns away from his second hour class and toward the gym.

I'm thinking about following him when the bell rings. I hurry up the stairs and slide into my seat in class just in time.

Sitting in class, I have a hard time paying attention to the lesson. I keep thinking about Hunter.

Last time I caught Hunter acting hinky at school he was drinking and doing drugs behind my back. I remember at the hospital when he said normally he would get shit-faced too handle what happened to his mom.

Mr. Traynor is super strict about cell phone use so mine is tucked in my bag. Most teachers at Pacific High don't give a shit if someone is on their phone. The attitude at the school is mostly like that of a college, the teachers say. In other words, if you want to be a dumb ass and on your phone instead of paying attention in class, you live with the consequences of an F.

If you can do it and pass the class, fine, too.

I like that attitude. But Mr. Traynor does not have that. Although I bitch about his rules with all my friends, I'm secretly glad. It makes it so I have to pay attention in math.

Usually. It's not working today, though.

I'm so anxious about him I consider telling Mr. Traynor that I don't feel good and leaving class so I can text Hunter. I talk myself out of it. I'm not his keeper. I'm his girlfriend, but he's a big boy. He can handle himself. And the reality is if he is off drinking right now—at ten in the morning—then there is little I can do to help him. Or stop him.

As soon as class is out, I get my phone out of my bag. My heart sinks. There are four messages. From Paige and Coral. None from Hunter.

Fuck. I open the first one from Paige. I know she has cheerleading practice this hour near the gym. I feel a knot in my stomach. It gets worse as I read.

"Fight in the gym. It's bad. Hunter and a couple of Josh's dicks. There's blood."

I open up the next one from Coral.

"Hunter got suspended." Coral works in the office second hour helping the secretary take attendance.

"Fuck," I say it out loud. A group of what looks like freshman shoot me startled looks.

"Sorry," I say. I race walk to the office, trying to squeeze through the massive crowd of kids in the hall during passing.

Finally, I'm at the door to the office. The principal's office is through the front office.

I rush inside. Coral isn't there anymore. The woman behind the desk smiles.

"Hi Kennedy," she says.

She's always been nice to me. Even after I got suspended for fighting. That time I attacked Carly. I think she felt bad for me because she heard me crying about hating myself for doing it.

I look past her at the principal's office door. It's some ways down the inner hall but I can tell the door is closed. I see dark shapes moving behind the frosted glass.

She sees where I'm looking. Before I can say anything, Mr. West bursts through the door. He has on jeans and a black button down shirt. If he wasn't so intimidating I'd think he was really handsome. For a dad.

His eyes flick over me and I know for sure he doesn't like me. He nods at me and strides right past the secretary's desk to the principal's office where he doesn't knock. He just opens the door. And then it's shut again and I hear raised voices.

The secretary smiles again. "Want to have a seat?"

I nod, grateful that she's not making me explain why I'm there. It's pretty damn obvious.

A few seconds later a woman with a beige suite and high heels and a man in a three-piece suit rush in. They give their names to the secretary. I recognize both names as the same last name as two of the football players.

"Right this, way," the secretary says and stands to escort them to the principal's office. This time when the door opens I catch a glimpse of Hunter's long legs in boots stretched out.

I hear more loud voices and then the nurse rushes past us from the other end of the inner hallway. She's carrying a pile of gauze and something else. I stand, alarmed.

"I think it's just a bloody nose," the secretary says. I sink back down to my chair.

It's got to be Hunter. I mean, he's obviously outnumbered here if he's in there with two football players.

Finally, the door opens and the woman in the heels and the man in the suit come out. Two football players I recognize trail behind them. They are huge dudes. They are the ones who were at the bonfire with Josh.

Their parents are talking to each other. Obviously, friends. Their backs are to us as the football players pass. One of them smirks. The other does something disgusting with his tongue when he sees me.

"Fuck off," I say.

The woman in the heels gasps. She turns and looks at me.

"Why don't you show your mama what you just showed me, tough guy?" I say.

"Haven't you ruined enough lives already," she says. To me. "You're his little tramp girlfriend who lied about Josh Masters. Do you realize you got him kicked off the football team, then kicked out of school? His scholarships were withdrawn and you've most likely ruined any future he might have had."

Now the guy in the suit has turned to and the look on his face is one of disgust.

I feel the rage swell inside me. "Excuse me?" I say and stand. I point my finger at her and it's shaking. "Listen, lady, you're the one who raised this perverted bully who likes to hang out with rapists. In my book, that makes you disgusting."

And I'm not even close to done. "And Josh deserves way worse than what he got. Do you think if someone tried to rape you, that them getting kicked off the football team and kicked out of school would be enough punishment? I doubt it!"

Unfortunately, during this exchange, I didn't hear the door open and realize that Hunter and his dad and the principal are all standing there. They heard every fucking word.

The woman and man walk out with a huff and the football players follow, but not before one of them turns to me and licks his lip. I want to barf.

I hear a shout and Hunter is lunging for him but his dad yanks him back by the shoulder.

"Dad!" He roars. "Let me at him!" That's when I realize with horror that Hunter's face is a massive bruise. He has two black eyes and his nose is red and swollen and he's clutching a blood-soaked wad of gauze.

His dad is restraining him with both arms now, clutching him in some type of wrestling grip. Hunter is trying to get away but failing.

His dad's voice cuts right through me as if it's being amplified through a megaphone, a sheer blast of fury. "Goddamn it, Hunter. You need to grow up, Son. Fighting over a girl is childish. You are ruining your future. Over a girl!"

The words echo in the room. Finally, Mr. West releases Hunter.

"Let's go," he says over his shoulder and heads toward the door.

My mouth is wide open. First that mother accuses me of ruining Josh Master's future and then Mr. West implies I'm the cause of ruining Hunter's future.

But Hunter comes to me. I reach for his face but don't touch it. It looks like it hurts.

"Are you okay?" I ask in a soft voice.

He shrugs. "I was outnumbered."

"You think?"

"They were the only two who got caught. There were three others."

"Jesus, Hunter."

"Hunter!" his dad roars from the open doorway.

Hunter ignores him completely.

Out of the corner of my eye I see his dad huff and slam the door shut. But before it closes he says, "If you're not home in twenty minutes, there will be hell to pay."

Again, Hunter ignores him.

"You better go," I say, but I'm reluctant to have him leave.

"Can you come over after school?" he says.

I scrunch my face. "What about your dad?"

He shrugs. "I don't care what he says. I just want to see you."

I nod.

He walks out.

The secretary gives me a sympathetic look, which somehow makes me feel worse.

I turn to leave. I have such mixed emotions. But the strongest one right now is hatred.

I hate Mr. West. I didn't want to admit it, but I fucking hate the guy. All I've ever done is love his son. And apparently, that's the worst thing I could be doing.

Fuck him.

## 8

M y first instinct is to go straight to Hunter's house. With my backpack hoisted on my shoulder, I head straight to my minivan in the parking lot, but when I text Hunter that I'm on the way, he immediately responds.

"I know I asked you to come, but now I think it's a bad idea. My dad is being a total dick. He wants to have some big talk when we get home. He has a meeting at the studio at four so come right after school."

I agree. Even though it's agony to wait. Plus, I'm anxious to hear the story from Hunter's mouth. All I get are tidbits from my friends: How Hunter and the football players were fighting in the gym.

It's torture to sit through the rest of my classes. Especially when I hear people whispering. They give me smiles, but they still shut up when I walk up or walk by in the halls. Dex and Devin aren't in class, Coral texts me.

"I'm worried." She says.

"Bout what?"

"Retaliation. Douchebags ganged up on Hunter. They want to fight back."

"Bad idea."

"Tell me about it."

In last hour, she texts me, "Phew. They are out at the basketball court taking out their frustration there. Dex finally got back to me. He's pissed."

"Me too," I write.

After school, I stop at the pizza place before I go to Hunter's place.

When I pull up I don't see his dad's Range Rover in the driveway and am relieved. It could be in the garage, but he often doesn't park it in the garage until he's home late at night for the night.

He must've left for his meeting already.

Hunter's door is unlocked so I try to sneak up the stairs but he's at the top of the stairs waiting.

"Oh, my God," he says, grabbing the pizza from me at the same time he kisses me. "You are the best girlfriend in the universe."

"Don't you forget it," I say.

He sets the pizza down and we hug. As we do, he winces. I draw back in alarm.

"Hunter!"

"it's nothing. I cracked some ribs. My dad took me to urgent care."

"Why didn't you tell me?"

He shrugs. "I didn't want you to worry. I wanted to see what the doctor said. It sort of felt like a punctured lung, but it's not. At first, it hurt like hell."

"Oh no. Are you in pain right now?"

"Nah. I'm on some good painkillers."

I squint. He's in AA. I'm not sure painkillers are a good idea, but what do I know?

I lift his shirt. He has bandages wound around his ribcage.

"You sure? You're sure you're okay?" I ask and swallow a lump of fear. I hate violence so much. It makes me sick to my stomach. Like I want to lean over and barf knowing that those two dickwads did that to Hunter.

He nods. "Yeah. My mouth kind of hurts though so don't think I'm a baby if I use a fork to cut my pizza."

"I suppose having wild and crazy sex right now would be out of the question?" I ask. I'm teasing.

He smiles.

"Oh, there's plenty of things that don't hurt right now."

"Huh?" I say. "Maybe I'll have to poke around and find exactly which *things* don't hurt?"

"Excellent idea," he says.

"First, what the fuck happened today?"

"I was walking to class and I got a text that said Carl and Maynard were in the gym talking about how they were going to hold you down and fuck your eye sockets," he shoots me a glance. "To be blunt."

I wave my hand. "Those losers wouldn't know what to do with an eye socket if they had one naked before them."

He laughs and I'm glad.

"So?" I prod.

"Then I got another text. They were talking about how you and Josh fucked or something."

I feel rage rise in me. He sees my face.

"I know,' he says and keeps talking "I just lost my mind and went to the gym and ... shoved Maynard up against the wall and next thing I know Carl and Marc and Brayden were on me and I was basically getting the shit beat of me. Then the coach came and broke it up. You saw me after that."

"Yeah,' I say. "You're lucky you weren't hurt worse. That was a totally unfair fight. Four guys on one? And how come only two of them got suspended? What happened to the other two?"

He gives me a look and shrugs. "Yeah, not fair. Next time I'll make sure the odds are even."

"Hunter," I say, "there can't be a next time. They could kill you. Just ride it out. We only have a few more months until graduation and you never have to see them again. Ever."

"Let's talk about what hurts and what doesn't," he says, training his eyes on me and reaching for me.

～

BEFORE I LEAVE LATER, I turn to him. "You have to ignore him," I say. "They want you to freak out. They want you to lose your temper and fight them, Hunter. You can't let them manipulate you that way."

He just stares at me.

"Hunter?"

His face shuts closed. His expression is unreadable.

"They're not worth it," I finally say and walk out. "You can't afford to risk your Fulbright Scholarship."

He makes a face. He knows I'm right. But even so, he mumbles, "How do you even know I'm going to accept it."

"You are," I say.

I can't control him. That's a fact. And I'm okay with it. I'm not his mother. But I still have a very bad feeling about it.

## 9

That night is a rare night when we are all home at dinnertime.

To celebrate, my mom makes my favorite—white sauce lasagna with huge thick slices of buttery garlic bread.

Oscar and I are mocking swoon as we chew.

"Damn, Justine," he says, pushing his empty plate away. "If book-keeping doesn't work out for you, maybe you should open a restaurant."

She grins. "You're on."

I smile at both of them. It's so awesome to see my mom so light at heart. She's back to the mom I knew when I was a little girl. My dad tried to crush her spirit. And he lost. I hate him. I never wanted to see him again.

But for some reason my mom didn't think this was a good idea. I didn't get it. He almost killed her. He ruined her life for years. And yet?

A few nights before that, my mom had come and knocked on my bedroom door. She was in her nightgown, robe and slippers. I was sitting at my desk doing homework.

"Have a sec?"

I smile. I still can't get over how great it is to have my mom in the same house. Even though we only lived apart for a few months, it felt like forever. I don't think I'd ever taken my mom for granted, but being apart from her for so long ensured I never would.

She came in and sat on the edge of my bed.

"I got a letter from your dad today."

My eyes narrowed and I scowled. Hearing that was enough to send me spiraling into a bad mood. How dare he write her? As far as I was concerned he was dead.

I waited. Her palm smoothed the bedspread down as she spoke, keeping her eyes on me.

"He's been sober for nine months now."

"Yeah. Because he can't get booze in prison, Mom," I say, exasperated. "Does he want to fucking award or something."

"Kennedy," my mom says and closes her eyes as if she is weary.

"I'm sorry for swearing, but why is he even writing you?"

"He wants me to forgive him." Her eyes fly open wide.

"And?" I say, holding my breath.

"I have."

I stand and shake my head. "He doesn't deserve that."

She stands, too. "You're right," she says and surprises me. "He doesn't. But I do."

I frown. She keeps talking.

"I've been reading a lot about forgiveness," she says. "And the reason we forgive someone is not for them. It's a very selfish act. It's one hundred percent for us."

I sit down on the bed. "How's that?"

"Your anger and resentment toward someone doesn't ever hurt them. It only hurts you," she says.

"I don't believe that," I say. After all, the entire reason I refuse to forgive my dad is because I want him to suffer. I want to punish him.

I decide just to say this.

"You're saying that me not forgiving dad doesn't hurt him?"

She sighs. "Well, in that case, it's different," she says. "But say you are driving down the road and someone cuts you off and you have to slam on the brakes so you don't crash. You might swear and get super angry. You might even spend the rest of the day fuming about the idiot driver who cut you off, right?"

I smile. Totally.

She continues. "But do you think that driver gives you another thought? No way. But here you are getting your blood pressure raised and fuming and having all these negative emotions that don't even affect that other driver for one second."

"Okay," I say.

"So maybe me forgiving your dad might make him feel a lot better, but if it does happen to do that I don't give a shit," she says.

My eyes are wide. She never swears.

"I'm doing it for me," she says. "If it benefits the other person by chance, then so be it. Do you understand?"

I nod. "So, did you write him back? To forgive him."

Now she looks down.

"You called him?"

"I'm flying out to say it to his face."

I'm stunned. My mouth is wide open.

"And I want you to come with me."

I shake my head furiously. "No. No way. I don't ever want to see him again."

"Kennedy. I think you need to see him and speak to him face-to-face to let it go," she says. "You still have a lot of anger and I hate to see it."

I freeze when she says this. Is she talking about my violent outbursts? Does she think they stem from repressed anger?

When Hunter's ex-girlfriend, Carly Winters, showed up at Pacific High, Hunter felt bad for her because of her mental problems and said he wanted to personally break the news that we were dating in a gentle way. But he dropped the ball.

*Carly is standing there in the middle of the hall, stopping all traffic, with a horrified look on her face. She's surrounded by a posse of girls who are glaring at us. Carly's mouth is open, and tears are welling in her eyes.*

*Suddenly, thank God, Paige and Coral are at my side.*

*Hunter swings his head, and I see the look on his face. It's irritation and something else. But then his expression is stone. He exhales loudly.*

*Once Hunter is looking, Carly lets out a strangled cry and is suddenly weeping loudly with her head in her hands. Her girls surround her, concerned, patting her back in between shooting us dirty looks.*

*"Thought you were going to give her a heads up?" I say to Hunter while still staring at Carly's antics.*

*He shakes his head. "Yeah. Didn't go as planned. I texted her and told her I wanted to meet and talk in person, but she ignored it."*

*"Fuck." Inside I was thinking well played, bitch.*

*And Paige and Coral must have thought the same thing.*

*"And the Oscar goes to Carly Winters," Coral says dryly.*

*I'm thinking it can't get any worse or more dramatic when Carly suddenly looks up, eyes dry, tosses her hair back and marches over to us. Before either one of us can react, she slaps Hunter across the face.*

*And I don't know what happens, but I instinctually spring.*

*It is like something primal has taken me over and I see my rage as if it is a living, breathing thing—a red streak of fury. I'm instantly on her, knocking her backward. We both fall to the ground, me on top of her, and her head hits the floor with a sickening thud. People start to scream, and I jump off her, horrified. I stand there in shock with my mouth open. Everyone gathers around her. I can barely see through the crowd but see them lift her to a sitting position. Her eyes are open but she is clearly dazed. Hunter is holding me tightly. My legs feel so weak that I think his grip is keeping me from falling.*

*I'm still in a stupor when teachers and the nurse appear and take Carly out of there. At the same time, I feel a hand on my arm. It's the principal. I'd only seen his picture in the hall. He leads me into the office, and I explain what happened. I vaguely remember Hunter watching us walk away with a horrified look on his face.*

*They took Carly to the hospital and suspended me.*

Carly ended up being okay. Physically. But then she went off the deep end and kidnapped me and drugged me and ended up back in a mental hospital.

Based on my violent reaction, I decided to seek therapy.

After I hurt Carly in a blind rage, I realized that my deepest fear was being violent like my dad. My therapist has helped a lot, but that phobia still rears its head every once in a while.

I've never really confessed this fear to my mom. She sees the look on my face now and gives me a sympathetic look.

"I know that's a lot to think about. You don't have to make a decision right now," she says and puts her hand on the bedroom doorknob. "Just think about it."

She leaves. The surge of anger that wells up inside me is mixed with an emotion I don't even want to admit to myself, but finally do: Sorrow.

My dad broke my heart.

I'm not going to give him the chance to do it again.

## 10

The next day at school I'm outraged to see the two football players, Carl and Maynard, in the hall before school. They have a group of guys gathered around them. I don't really notice them until I'm practically on top of them. They spread out and block my way.

I can feel my face redden.

They all stand there staring at me. It's grown suddenly quiet.

I stand across from them in a face off. I instinctively stand in a defensive pose. I took a self-defense class last summer before I moved to California. Some of it is foggy, but some of it is crystal clear. I may be smaller and outnumbered, but I can still do some damage.

My hands are by my side. They're shaking.

For some reason defending myself doesn't feel like violence. It feels like survival. So even though my deepest darkest fear is being a violent person like my father, self-defense feels like something entirely different.

But it still doesn't stop me from wanting to barf.

Pull it together, Kennedy. That simple phrase stops the shaking and makes me stand straighter.

Carl notices and his eyes squint slightly.

"Get the fuck out of my way," I say.

"We aren't going to hurt you sweet thing," Maynard says. "Unless you beg us to."

"That's right," Carl says. "We just want to taste some of that sweet nectar." He runs his tongue around his lips. Josh said you taste like a peach."

I stare stonily at them. Off to one side I see Emma and Paige out of the corner of my eye, but I don't take my eyes off the boys in front of me.

"We can make you feel real good," Maynard says. "Once you had the real thing baby you'll never go back."

The bell rings. I see Emma take off running down the hall with Paige. They're going to get help. I know they're not running to class.

"If you don't move and let me pass I'm going to go down the line and kick each one of you in the nuts," I say and then smile.

They exchange glances and start to laugh.

Until I walk up to Carl and plant my boot, not in his crotch, but on that spot where his ankle meets his foot. He crumples in a heap on the floor howling. Before anyone can react, I've stomped on Maynard's foot next to him.

Maynard doesn't go down, though. He swings at me. I duck, but he manages to grab a hunk of my hair and yanks me toward him.

Just then I hear a scream like a banshee and hear feet running behind me. It's Dex and Devin and some other guys.

Right then, a teacher steps out of the nearest classroom. She's an older woman with gray hair and glasses and she takes in what's going on instantly. Her eyes flicker from Carl on the ground, to me bent over, held tight by Maynard's death grip on my scalp.

"Let go of her right this instant."

Maynard releases my hair and I back up, just as the teacher steps right between the football players and Dex and Devin who just arrived red-faced and panting.

"I'm going to kill you," Devin says, trying to go around the teacher. She puts a palm on his chest.

"Now, now."

"What the hell?" It's the principal. He's right behind me.

He comes up and thumps Dex and then Devin on the head with his palm and then strides past me and pokes all five boys facing me in the chest.

I hear assorted complaints. "Ow." "You can't do that, dude." "Fuck."

The principal ignores them and just lifts his arm and points to the office.

But the teacher stops him. She points to Dex and Devin. "These two young men just arrived at the same time I did. They were, like me, just coming to this young lady's rescue."

The principal finally notices me standing there.

The teacher continues. "You might want to have her checked out. I think Maynard Cross might have taken a fistful of hair out of her scalp. At least it looked that way to me."

"She stomped on my foot," Carl said in a whining voice.

The principal turned to him and rolled his eyes. "My office. Now."

I stand there as the four of them head to the office. The principal turns to me. "I think you should probably come, too."

I nod. Why not? I might as well just have my own desk there at this point.

Paige is at my side. "You okay?"

I nod. "Yeah. Thanks."

IN the office, I tell the principal what happened with my arms folded over my chest. He's not my friend. But he needs to hear what happened.

When I tell them I stomped on Carl's foot, he doesn't blink.

I finish and he says, "Well, if you don't think you need the nurse to check you out, you're excused."

He looks down and shuffles some papers.

I stay seated.

He looks back up and raises an eyebrow.

I meet his eyes. "I hope you suspend them this time. When you let them get away with ganging up on Hunter West, you basically gave them a free pass to bully anyone. Including someone two feet shorter and one hundred pounds lighter."

He doesn't answer. I stand and walk out leaving his door wide open.

I keep my head held high as I walk past the four goons sitting in the other room.

The halls have emptied. I'm late for my class and they didn't give me a pass but I don't care.

I'm nearly there when my phone dings. Hunter.

"I'm outside."

I look around as if I can see him from inside the halls. My heart is pounding.

"Where?" I write.

"My spot."

He usually parks his Jeep in the same spot. Most people leave it open for him.

"Be right there," I write.

I turn around and head back toward the front of the school.

In seconds, I'm outside and making my way toward the side parking lot.

He's leaning against his Jeep.

"Will you get in trouble for being here?" I say as I get closer, looking around.

He shrugs and then spits. "I don't give a fuck."

His face has an expression I've never seen. He looks like he's about to murder someone.

"I guess you heard," I say.

"Damn right, I did."

I can practically feel the heat waves rolling off him.

"It's fine. I handled it."

His eyes flick to me and then past me.

"They need to learn."

It's almost as if I'm not even there and he's just talking to himself. He's staring over my shoulder. I turn and see the four football players pile into a big Cadillac Escalade. Looks like one of the parents picked them all up.

I turn back around.

"Hunter? Learn what?"

"Learn that if they ever mess with you again I'll kill them."

## 11

I talk Hunter into taking me to lunch at the taco stand on a bluff overlooking the ocean. All my girls have been texting me nonstop. I did a group text to fill them in and said I was skipping school.

After we eat, I turn to Hunter "What do you want to do?"

He's been quiet most of lunch. I can tell he's still fuming.

I reach out and hold his hand. "It's fine, Hunter. They are just bullies. And wimps. I mean what kind of idiot gets off on intimidating a female way smaller than him? Total loser. Probably super insecure."

Wrong thing to say.

He stands and takes our paper plates and napkins to the trash.

What a buzz kill he is. I understand he's mad, but he needs to just let it go.

"They aren't worth it," I say and realize I've said this numerous times lately. Even I'm getting sick of hearing it.

"My mom got out of the hospital," he says unemotionally.

"That's great news," I say. "Where is she?"

He looks down and then shrugs.

Fuck.

"I thought she said she was going back to detox at Palm Springs?"

"I thought so, too."

"I'm sorry," I say.

"Whatever."

He stalks off to the Jeep. I hate how cold and emotionless he is. It scares me.

We go back to my place and he doesn't want to have sex.

My mom isn't there and he uses that as an excuse.

"She could walk in any time."

It's true, but she would never walk into my room without knocking and besides, I could lock it.

But I don't argue. He heads for the living room, grabs the remote and plops on the couch watching sports.

Really?

I'm trying to be understanding but I'm starting to get irritated. The last thing I want to do is watch sports on TV. After a while, he leans his head back and is asleep. I wonder if he slept at all last night.

While he sleeps, I creep over to the counter and open my laptop. I work on some homework until he wakes again.

He stretches and yawns loudly and then checks his phone. He stares at it for a few seconds and then stands. "I better go. I'm supposed to have dinner with my dad tonight."

My feelings are hurt. He was a total drag to be around all day. He barely paid any attention to me and was crabby and closed off. And now he bails to eat dinner with his dad. I have to admit that part of it is because it stings to never be invited to anything that involves his dad. That guy must really hate me. I can't figure it out.

Hunter gives me a sweet kiss at the door and then is gone.

## 12

I'm starting to get ready for bed when Coral calls.

Calls. Not messages. Not texts.

Because of this, my heart is racing as I answer.

She doesn't wait for me to say hello.

"I can't get ahold of Dex," she says.

"Okay?"

"I was just out at Jack's Pizza and ran into Ava. She was picking up four large pizzas to go. One of her posse of girls was whispering and said something about the boys 'needing a good meal after the ass kicking they're going to give.' And she looks right at me."

"Oh, fuck."

"I called Dex. No answer. I texted. Same. So, I called and texted Devin and he didn't answer, either. I drove straight to their houses and their SUV was gone."

As Coral speaks, I'm reaching into my closet to pull on a sweatshirt and leggings, shedding my flannel pajama pants as I do.

"Then—"

"You went to Hunters," I interrupt. "And they were there, either."

Hunter's Jeep was gone.

"Fuck."

"Where do you think they are?" she asks.

I pause. "The beach or the basketball court."

"I'm at the beach," she says. "I'll meet you at the basketball court."

I'm already out the door and starting my minivan.

I didn't leave a note for Mom or Oscar but they can text me if they're worried.

Right now, I'm too freaked out.

I'm afraid of what will happen when Josh and his friends meet up with Hunter and his. It's going to be bad. Really bad. I wonder if I should call 911.

Coral calls and we talk the entire drive.

"I'm sick to my stomach," she says.

"Me, too."

"I'm almost there."

"Me, too."

As soon as I pull into the parking lot I see two dozen cars or so at the far end near the basketball courts and baseball fields. It's pretty dark but I with the streetlights I can see a bunch of people gathered in the middle of the baseball field.

Coral's car pulls in right behind me. I pull partway onto the field and jump out, heading toward the dugout. I can hear shouting and screams now.

I push my way through the crowd with both hands, physically shoving people out of my way to clear a path. Coral is on my heels. When we get close to the center, all I see is a mass of bodies wrestling and throwing punches.


TWO GUYS ARE on the ground, grappling and throwing punches. I'm searching for Hunter. It's really dark so I can barely make out Hunter, but I manage to tell which one of the fighting bodies is Hunter. Of course, he's squared off with some huge football player. They are leaning into one another throwing punches like it's a boxing match. They then part and back off and go for it again. Hunter manages to loop an arm around the guy's neck and is punching him in the face when I hear Coral let loose with a blood curdling scream right beside me.

Someone is standing over a kid on the ground kicking him in the face.

Everything stops and it grows quiet as Coral screams and runs toward the two.

The dark figure freezes, boot in mid-kick. Coral is kneeling down now. I'm right behind her, my eyes straining in the dark until I realize who it is. It's Dex.

I look up, but whomever was kicking him is gone. Everyone is running away.

She's wailing and crying and cradling his head. Then she looks up wild-eyed and screams. "Call 911! Call 911!"

Most people are racing out of the parking lot in their vehicles. I look around wild-eyed and reach for my phone. I punch in the numbers and shakily tell the dispatcher we need an ambulance. Someone is badly hurt.

I give our location and say, "Hurry! Now! Hurry! Please!"

The dispatcher assures me someone is coming and asks for my number to call back.

I give it to her. Devin is on his knees now beside Dex. Hunter is standing above them with his head in his hands.

I rush over to Coral. "They're coming."

I'm afraid to look down at Dex. His eyes are not open. He looks dead.

Hunter starts shouting and swearing.

Coral looks up at him and says in a cold voice, "Dex didn't even want to fight. He told me he hoped he didn't have to fight for you. But he's so goddamn loyal to you, Hunter!"

Hunter reels back as if he's been punched.

Sirens in the distance break the moment. I rush over to the parking lot, which has completely emptied now except for our four cars. Motherfuckers.

I stand at the edge of the field waving my arms frantically until the ambulance stops in front of me.

"Over here!"

They rush over to Dex.

The rest is a blur. I remember Hunter is standing on the periphery of everything swearing and pulling at his hair. I know I should go over to him, but I can't leave Coral's side. She has a death-grip on my hand.

They load Dex into the ambulance. In the light, I see he has tubes hooked up everywhere. Devin climbs in the back and the doors slam.

"I'll drive you," I say and rush Coral to my minivan.

When I turn to look for Hunter, his Jeep is gone.

Fuck.

But I can't let Coral go. She needs me right now. I wish Hunter would have come to me. I would drive him, as well.

He shouldn't be driving right now.

Nothing makes sense. Everything seems surreal. We speed to the hospital staying behind the ambulance. When we pull into the emergency circle drive, I see Hunter's Jeep parked sideways and he is at the doors waiting. When they unload Dex, he and Devin are at the EMT's side as they wheel the gurney in.

Coral jumps out and races after them.

I know I can't park there. As much as I want to just ditch my car and run in, if I do, I'll block the way for another ambulance.

It takes me a few minutes to find the hospital parking garage and then I run to the emergency room entrance.

There are a few people in the E.R.: a burly guy sitting in the corner staring at me. A mother with a baby in a stroller and a toddler in her arms. An elderly couple holding hands. A guy in a flannel shirt holding his hand that is wrapped in what looks like several white shirts.

My friends are seated on a couch in a corner.

I run over. Hunter looks up at me with a stricken look on his face.

Coral is weeping. Devin has his arm around her.

"How?"

"They don't know anything, yet."

"Oh, my God." I sink into the chair beside Hunter and reach for his hand.

He jerks his hand away and stands, pacing.

Coral glares at him.

I shoot her a questioning look and she glares at me.

Jesus.

We sit like this for what feels like hours. Finally, a doctor or nurse or somebody comes out. Hunter, who is still pacing, freezes.

"He's stable," the nurse says. He turns to Devin. "Can we talk?"

My heart sinks. Coral bursts out in fresh tears.

The doctor leads Devin down the hall.

Hunter comes and sits down, leaning over putting his head in his hands.

Coral lifts her head and stares at him as if willing him to look up. When he does, she says, "If he's not okay, you know this is your fault."

"Coral!" I say, jumping up. "That's not true and that's not fair. Hunter didn't make Dex do anything."

"Stay out of this," Coral says in a low voice laced with venom.

I meet her eyes and say, "The ones at fault here are the guy who did this to Dex and Josh Masters."

She looks away. I walk over to sit beside her. She jumps up, recoiling as if I've burned her.

"You're wrong, Kennedy," she says in that same deadly voice. "It's your fault. And Hunter's fault. If you guys hadn't started all this shit with Josh."

Fury rages through me. I jump up, too and can feel my face getting hot as I say, "This shit? This shit? You mean how Josh Masters attempted to rape me. I started that? Fuck you, Coral. Fuck you."

I'm about to grab Hunter's hand and take off. Where? I don't know. But somewhere far away from Coral. Otherwise I might slap her face.

But the return of Devin, alone, stops me.

He has been crying.

"He's in a coma," he says. "They are keeping him that way because he has brain swelling. They don't know anything right now."

He sits down by Coral and she reaches for him, holding him in her arms.

At the same time, Hunter jumps up and takes a wild swing. I hear a crunch as his fist sinks through the plaster on the greenish painted wall. Blood springs up on his knuckles and is flying everywhere as he swings again shouting, "I'm going to kill him!"

Before his fist connects again, a hand grabs his arm.

It's the big burly guy who was sitting in the corner looking ominous.

"That's enough," the guy grumbles.

Hunter looks at him wild-eyed and then turns and storms out of the emergency room doors. I am running after him, but by the time I get outside, his Jeep is squealing out of the circle drive.

## 13

I watch his taillights disappear and then it hits me.

HE'S GOING after Josh and somebody is going to die.

I RACE to the parking garage.

ONCE, when I first moved here, we'd driven by Josh's house and Emma had pointed it out.

Now, I speed out of the parking lot onto the main road heart pounding and palms sweaty. "Call Hunter!" I shout at my phone. But it goes straight to voice mail. "Text Hunter!"

"Please call me." I say.

Nothing.

After about ten minutes I pull down a back road in the hills above Malibu. I look at the address as I pull in. This can't be right. The main house is huge and dark. But then I see a small drive leading to one side and lights on and cars parked. A guest house.

WHEN I PARK, I don't see Hunter's Jeep. Instead there is a group of girls huddled near the front door. I race up.

"IS JOSH HERE?"

THEY ALL TURN. I'm face to face with Ava.

"WELL, WELL, MY HAVE THINGS CHANGED," she says.

"FUCK OFF, AVA," I say. "This is serious."

SOMETHING FLICKERS ACROSS HER FACE—IT looks like doubt.

"IS DEX?" her voice cracks a little.

I SHAKE MY HEAD. "We don't know. His brain is swollen. He's in a coma."

AGAIN, something flashes across her eyes.

"WHY DO YOU WANT JOSH?" Her voice is cold. Her bitchy friends are all staring at me.

. . .

"Can I talk to you alone for a minute?"

She bites her lip, considering and then nods. I head back toward my car.

"What is it, bitch?"

"I'm worried. Hunter left the hospital and I think he's going after Josh. I'm scared. I need to stop him. And I need your help."

She stares at me for a few seconds. And then she reaches for the door handle to my passenger side door. "Get in."

As soon as she is sitting, she fiddles with her phone and then looks up at the group of girls. They all check their phones and then head toward their cars.

She doesn't speak as I pull the main road except to give directions. "Turn here. Take the next left. Finally, we pull into an area high up in the Hollywood Hills. The road leading up a steep hill has a guard shack and security vehicle parked out front. The guard just looks at us as we pass.

The road is dotted with homes and driveways on the steep hillside overlooking the city. The lights of L.A. look like a magical fairyland beyond them. Ava tells me to pull over at a huge modern house. As I pull up, I can see that most of the house is situated down the cliffside.

We pull into the circle drive facing the front and a massive glass window. Thick curtains hide what's inside, but light filters out.

SHE TURNS TO ME. "He's housesitting," she says. "Unfortunately, everybody knows he is because he's been posting it on social media."

I'M LISTENING to her but looking frantically around for Hunter's Jeep. I don't see it.

"IF EVERYONE KNOWS THEN he needs to leave. At least for the night. Until I can find Hunter and calm him down. I'm worried he's going to kill Josh, Ava."

I DON'T KNOW why I tell her this and instantly regret it.

SHE HAS OPENED my door and is nearly out. "I'll make him come to my house for the night."

I NOD and exhale in relief.

SHE STARES at me for a few seconds and then says, "Thanks. Where's Hunter now? You better go find him."

IT'S SO SINCERE. I look over and she looks worried.

"WAIT? Are you worried about Hunter or Josh?"

. . .

SHE LOOKS AWAY. "I'm not doing this for Josh."

"Is that what all of this is about? Why you hate me so much?" I say. "Because you're still in love with Hunter?"

SHE LOOKS me straight in the eyes. "I'm not love in Hunter."

"OKAY," I say. "Can you at least tell me why you're helping then?"

HER EYES NARROW. "I'm not telling you anything. Don't mistake my gratefulness for friendship, bitch."

THEN SHE SLAMS THE DOOR.

I KNOW I should go home to bed, but I pull over on the shoulder a little bit below the house. I'm not sure why. I guess I want to wait to make sure Hunter doesn't show up before they leave. After about ten minutes, I see Josh's Porsche speed down the road past me.

THANK GOD. I'm about to start the van to leave when I see Hunter's Jeep zoom past me. He and Josh must've just missed each other on the turnoff below.

BEFORE I CAN REACT, Hunter has pulled to a stop and jumped out. He stands before the modern looking house holding something dark and long in both hands. Holy shit. It's a gun. I watch as he fires and the huge glass front window explodes.

LIGHTS FLASH on at the house next door. Hunter fires again. And then just as I hear sirens nearby, he jumps in his car and heads further up the hill.

The private security vehicle has its lights and siren on as it speeds past me and after Hunter's Jeep. Fuck.

MORE LIGHTS FLICK ON.

I PULL onto the road and follow. At the top of the hill, this road tees at a larger road. I don't know which way to turn. I'm too late.

ONLY THEN DO I go home.

I CRAWL into bed near dawn. Hunter still hasn't returned my messages. Neither has Coral. Devin has only responded to say, "He's the same."

I AM sick with worry but somehow, I manage to fall asleep.

THE NEXT MORNING, I wake close to noon. Nobody has called me back. I text Hunter again and say the same thing, "Please call."

AFTER MY SHOWER, I get a text from Devin. "He's awake. He's going to be okay. The swelling is gone."

·   ·   ·

I TYPE "THANK GOD. On my way."

THEN I WRITE, "Have you heard from Hunter."

HE WRITES BACK, "NO."

I PUT down my phone and start bawling with relief. And then it turns into worry. Where the fuck is Hunter?

I TEXT PAIGE.

"HAVE YOU TALKED TO CORAL?"

"AT HOSPITAL WITH HER NOW."

I SWALLOW. I wonder if Coral is still mad at me and Hunter. I hope now that Dex is okay, she's over it.

"HAVE YOU TALKED TO HUNTER?"

"*NADA*," she writes.

"ON MY WAY."

. . .

As soon as I hit send I start bawling. I'm hyperventilating and have snot and tears running down my face. I clean myself up and dress to go to the hospital.

Downstairs there's a note from my mom. She's over at the neighbors doing bookkeeping work. I scribble on the note, "Be back later."

With my keys in my hand, I step outside.

Hunter's Jeep is parked in my driveway. He's slumped in the front seat.

I rush over and yank open his door. He's breathing. And it smells like booze. And vomit. I see he's puked all over himself. I shake his shoulder.

"Hunter?"

He leans over and vomits on the floorboard, blinking.

"Come on," I say. "Let's get you inside."

He leans on me and I basically walk him into the main floor guest bedroom. I steer him toward the shower.

. . .

HE LOOKS at me with bloodshot eyes. "Dex?"

HE DOESN'T KNOW. "He's awake. He's okay."

THEN MY BIG tough boyfriend collapses on the bed and cries. He's angrily wiping his tears away. I climb onto the bed with him and hug him, kissing his hair over and over and telling him it's going to be okay.

"I'M STILL DRUNK, KENNEDY," he says.

"I KNOW."

"I DON'T WANT to be a drunk."

"I KNOW," I say. "Let's get you in the shower."

I HELP him strip and then put him in the shower. I stay in the bathroom to make sure he doesn't pass out. He gets out and wraps a towel around himself and stumbled to the bed.

IN A FEW SECONDS, he's snoring.

I SIT in a chair and watch YouTube videos on my phone. I'm trying to keep my mind off of all the shit that I'm going to have to deal with soon. This is a brief respite.

.   .   .

WHEN HE WAKES a few hours later, he sits up and moans. I hand him a plastic bottle of sports drink and an aspirin. "Can you keep this down?"

HE NODS AND DOWNS BOTH.

"LET'S GET YOU HOME. I'll drive your Jeep."

"COPS ARE AFTER ME."

"WHAT?"

"I SHOT up the house Josh was in with a BB gun."

"I KNOW," I say.

"THEY GOT MY LICENSE PLATE, I think. Can I leave my Jeep here?"

"HUNTER, if they have your license plate number, they know where you live."

"OH." Then he shakes his head. "I knew that."

.   .   .

THIS IS BAD. He's going to be arrested.

"HOW YOU FEELING?"

"BETTER."

I NOD. "You need to call your dad."

HE LOOKS DOWN AND NODS. He knows I'm right.

MR. WEST SHOWS up with some dude.

"GIVE Sam the keys to your Jeep, son."

HUNTER WORDLESSLY HANDS his keys over.

MEANWHILE, Mr. Big Douche Movie Director, aka Hunter's Dad, hasn't even looked at me, despite me being the one who opened the door. He walked right past me to where Hunter is standing in his vomit-stained clothes.

HE HANDS HUNTER A BAG. "Go put these on." It must contain clean clothes.

. . .

HUNTER DISAPPEARS TOWARD THE BATHROOM. The guy named Sam walks out the front door.

AND I JUST STAND THERE STARING AT Mr. West.

DAMN IF I'M going to be the first one to speak.

FINALLY, he looks over at me.

BUT HE DOESN'T SAY anything. I vow not to be the first one to look away, but when Hunter walks in, I do.

HE IS in clean jeans and a shirt. He looks a lot better.

"LET'S GO."

"WHERE? WHAT?"

"I'LL EXPLAIN IN THE CAR."

HE TURNS TO LEAVE. Hunter ignores him and walks over to me and wraps me in his arms.

"YOUR DAD HATES ME," I say.

. . .

"It doesn't matter." He draws back and looks me in the eyes. "You know how I feel about you."

I nod. "Same."

Even though we've said we love each other before, it's still somewhat awkward to just say it causally. We both tend to avoid it. But I know what he means. And he knows what I mean.

"I'll call you."

I nod.

Then he is gone.

I stumble upstairs to my room and fall into bed.

In the morning, I reach for my phone.

There are several texts from Hunter. "I'm in L.A. My dad made me go to cops and confess shooting. They're investigating what happened to Dex. Bunch of football players there say they didn't see who hit him. More later."

"Fuck," I mumble.

. . .

WHEN I GET DOWNSTAIRS. I see Samantha sitting at the bar.

"HELLO, KENNEDY," Samantha says.

"SORRY," I say, looking up. "Do you know where my mom is?"

"IN THE LADIES' room." She twirls a glass of white wine that is on the counter in front of her.

THERE'S another glass beside it.

"COOL."

I TEXT HUNTER BACK. "Keep me posted."

"OKAY," he writes back. "Gtg." Got to go."

I POKE my head in the refrigerator to look for food when she says, "How is your boyfriend's mother?"

"HUH?" Then I remember she was there that day. "She's fine, thanks."

"OH, THAT'S A RELIEF."

.   .   .

I LOOK over and she's smiling. "I know that's tough. When your boyfriend or someone you care about has family issues, it inevitably affects you, right?"

I LOOK AT HER AGAIN. Maybe she isn't so bad. I nod. "Yeah."

THEN MY MOTHER WALKS IN. "Hi, honey!" She walks over and hugs me and I hug her tightly back. I want to tell her everything that happened, but not with Samantha here.

THEY START TALKING about something stupid, some TV show and then they turn it on. It's some reality TV show. I'm irritated. I wanted to spend time with my mom. I miss her. It's bad enough that she has to work for this weird woman, but she has to socialize with her, too?

I INSTANTLY FEEL guilty because I know my mom had complained when she first moved that it was hard to move here and make friends. And now she has one and I'm pissy about it.

LEANING over I kiss her cheek and say, "I'm going to go study."

"OKAY, HONEY."

I DON'T SAY goodbye to Samantha.

AND SHE DOESN'T SAY goodbye to me.

## 14

As soon as I wake early the next day I text Hunter.

"What's up?" I ask.

"Meeting with the DA later today. They got ahold of the house owner."

"Shit."

"I know."

"Are you on house arrest by your dad or can I come over?"

"Arrest."

"That sucks."

"Yeah, my dad is not happy."

"Let me know when I can see you. I miss you." I type. And then at the last minute I write. "Heard from Dex?"

"Yeah. He's okay. Getting sprung today, maybe."

"Oh, good."

I want to go see him, but I need to go to school. I'm worried about falling behind.

Miss Flora asks if we can reschedule the interview until after school and I agree.

I don't see any of my friends until lunch. When I walk up to where they are seated in the cafeteria, Coral gets up and walks out before I get there. Shit.

I sit down and want to cry. I push my tray of food away. But damn if I'm going to chase after her. She said some awful things.

Emma gives me a sympathetic look. "She'll get over it."

"Maybe," I say. Obviously, they already know we are fighting.

Paige nods. "She kind of hinted that she felt bad. But I think she's too stubborn to make the first move."

I smile wryly. "Same."

"Maynard, and Brayden are suspended because the police are investigating what they did to Dex."

"Good," I say. "What about the others?"

Paige shrugs. "Nobody's talking. Me and Hunter talked to the cops. His dad made us."

"I can talk to them," I say.

I stand and walk out and call the police station.

The woman who answers says she'll have the detective in charge call me back."

After school, I head to Miss Flora's class.

She gives me a big smile. "I'm so excited about this."

I smile but it feels fake.

We spend the next forty-five minutes just chatting. But the camera is on me the entire time. After a while, I forget about it. I really like Miss Flora and find it really easy to talk to her. However, when we wrap it up, I am suddenly self-conscious about what I revealed.

But it's too late now.

When I get home, I text Hunter. He hasn't texted all day.

"Did you meet with DA yet?" I write when he finally answers.

"Yeah. It's all good. The owner agreed not to prosecute if I go to A.A. I think there was some money that exchanged hands."

"I bet."

"Gtg. AA meeting starting in five."

"Miss you."

"I'll call you on my way home."

I work on my homework since I have a huge test in the morning. I study sitting at the kitchen counter while my mom watches TV with Oscar. They are laughing over some silly sitcom and it feels normal and natural and homey. I want to be around it instead of holed up in my room.

Two hours later my phone rings.

It's an unfamiliar number. I rush to answer it, grabbing my phone and heading out to the back deck. My mom gives me a surprised look. It's a Detective Reynolds. I breathlessly tell him everything I saw. When I'm done, he asks if I could see the people's faces who were beating up Dex. I frown and shake my head even though he can't see it.

"It was so dark..." I say and trail off. "But Coral she saw. She was up close."

"We did speak to a young lady by that name."

"Okay. Good," I say. "Are you going to make an arrest?"

"We're still investigating."

"Oh."

"If you can think of anything else please call back," he says.

I hang up feeling helpless. Then my phone rings. It's Hunter this time. I tell him what happened as I lean on the back rail and soak in the sunset and ocean breeze. The sunset is turning the ocean in front of me liquid gold.

"Yeah. I told them it was Josh, as well."

"Think they'll arrest him?"

"Dunno," Hunter says. "My dad says me and Coral seeing it might not be enough."

"That sucks," I say. We are both quiet. Then to change the subject I ask how his AA meeting was.

"Cool."

That makes me laugh. "Cool? Wasn't it a bunch of old dudes with big red noses?"

He laughs, but it doesn't seem genuine.

"Sorry," I say, immediately feeling awful. "That was insensitive."

"Nah, it's cool. It's actually a bunch of teen actors and stuff."

"Really?" I say. For some stupid reason, I'm jealous.

"Where is it? The meeting?"

"Hollywood. My dad insisted I go. It's right by his office at the studio. He thinks he needs to babysit me to make sure I go. So, I have to stop by his office every day before I go to the meeting to let him know I'm following through."

I make a face. "Every day?"

"Oh yeah. That's what the DA said. I have to go to a meeting every day for two months. That's my punishment."

"That sucks," I say.

I can hear him inhale sharply. "Kennedy, I got a break. They were talking about charging me with felony vandalism."

"Oh shit."

"I know."

"What about school?"

"Since it's for teenagers, it's right after school. I can leave and get there in time for the meeting. But because of traffic, I have to stick around for an hour or two and then head home. My dad says if I want I can hang out at his office. I'm working for him this summer on the set and he said there's some stuff I can learn now."

My heart sinks. When is there room for me? I glance at the clock. "It's nearly eight."

"I thought the meeting was right after school?"

"Well, sort of. It's at five. So, if I leave from school I can get there in time."

"Did the meeting just get out?"

He pauses before answering. Suddenly, I feel like a jealous girlfriend making him account for his time. I hate that feeling.

"It gets out at seven. We all went to dinner?"

"We?"

"Some of the kids in AA. They're pretty cool."

Now, I'm really jealous. I hate it. And I hate what I say next, but I say it anyway.

"Well, hope you can fit me in to your busy life, Hunter."

He's silent for a few seconds and then says, "Kennedy, you're the most important thing in my life. There's always room for you. Can I come over now?"

I have a big test to study for tomorrow. I hate to do it, but I have to say no. I explain about the test. "How about tomorrow after your meeting?"

"For sure," he says.

Then after a few minutes we hang up.

By now the sun has set and the air is suddenly cold, giving me goosebumps. I head inside and to my room to study.

Everything feels off with Hunter, but I can't think about it right now. Graduating with a good GPA is my focus right now. It has to be.

## 15

The next night I shower and put on perfume and a super cute new top for Hunter.

My mom and Oscar see how excited I am to see Hunter and discretely disappear to their rooms when he calls that he's on his way.

I throw open the door and hug him tight.

"Hey, gorgeous," he says.

All my misgivings from the night before disappear.

It feels so good to have him hold me. Nothing feels better.

I lead him by the hand out to the deck. It's dark but I've lit more than a dozen candles in holders on the deck.

"Wow," he says.

I lead him over to a double wide lounge chair covered with pillows and soft blankets. There is some sexy music playing from a speaker.

He swallows and turns to me. "Um, are Oscar and your mom home?"

"They aren't coming out here, trust me."

He reaches for me, but then stops. "I don't know. This is kind of weird."

I stand before him and press myself against him, wrapping my arms around his neck and kissing him deeply until he moans.

He pulls back. "Damn, Kennedy."

I smile.

Then I take his hand and lead him to the lounge chair.

"How was the meeting?"

His voice is full of excitement. "It's really cool. The kids are so cool. I mean some of their stories, holy shit? Like this one guy, Cruz, he has this fucked up story about thinking he could fly and then having someone catch him when He jumped and ..."

I'm tuning him out. I don't want to admit it but I'm insanely jealous of the excitement I hear in his voice.

"Kennedy?"

"Mmm?"

"Did you hear me?"

"Sorry."

"I was just saying I think that I can really do this. I think now that I've met a bunch of people like me who don't drink or do drugs anymore and really are dedicated to sticking to it, I can do it, too."

I nod, trying to be understanding and supportive but all I hear is "a bunch of people like me." What about me?

"That's great, Hunter." And then I put my finger on his lips to shush him and then grab him by the back of the head and bring him into me.

He is moaning in seconds. I'm glad he is excited about the AA meeting, but right now the only thing I want him to be excited about is me.

We are hot and heavy under the blankets when I smell cigarette smoke. I ignore it until I hear giggling. It's so weird. I sit up and look around.

Oh, God. It's that idiot neighbor, Samantha. She is leaning against the rail and there's a guy there with her. They are still twenty feet away but it feels like she's right beside me.

She sees me looking and takes the guy by the hand leading him inside.

Way to ruin the mood.

"Get back here, Kennedy," Hunter growls and pulls me toward him.

I crawl back under the blankets but tell him I'm suddenly uncomfortable with doing anything more than kissing.

He laughs but then says, "I could make out with you all night long."

After a while, though, we both lay back holding hands and watching the stars. It's one of the most romantic nights of my life.

When he kisses me goodbye and leaves, I hug myself. I'm the luckiest girl in the world.

But in the back of my mind, there is a dark shadow looming. The Fulbright.

## 16

After school, I head straight home. I'm planning on spending the entire night editing footage for film class. I can't wait. I love that for the first time in my entire school career, I'm finally doing something in the classroom that feels important. It feels as if I'm actually doing something that is going to help my career.

The house is empty when I get home. Oscar is shooting a commercial in the desert. My mom left a note on the counter that she's getting her hair done. That makes me smile, but also sad.

Because it triggers a shitty memory. It was when money was tight my mom had gone to get her haircut from a friend who had a salon in her basement.

*My mom returned home with her hair cut and curled and she just seemed to glow. She walked in smiling and giggly saying, "Sorry, I'm late. I spent some time catching up with Cathy after."*

*I had my purse on my shoulder and was about to leave to go to Sherie's house.*

*"Mom, you look so pretty."*

*And then my dad stood up from the couch. There was an empty bottle of something on the coffee table in front of him. When my mom saw him stand, her smile disappeared. I looked from my dad's face to my mom's.*

*"Please?" She was looking at my dad and then she nodded toward me. My dad looked at me and then pivoted so he wasn't heading toward her anymore. He went into the kitchen and then I heard the back door slam.*

*"Is everything okay?" I asked.*

*"It's fine. I'll handle it."*

*"Are you sure?" I said.*

*She gave me a bright smile. "Of course. I'll go talk to him. He probably just had a bad day and needs to talk about it."*

*I paused. I wasn't sure. But I also knew she'd told me numerous times that it wasn't my business. At the time, I didn't know that he hit her. I just knew they argued. She always hid the beatings from me. Until the last one.*

*What I did know was that when they argued, it was scary and my mom would sometimes take to bed the next day. At the time, I thought it was because she was depressed, but I know now she was hiding her physical injuries.*

*Once I realized he hit her, all the times she had told me she was klutzy and had gotten bruises from running into things or tripping came into sharp relief for what they really were.*

*On this day, I obliviously ran off to hang out with my friends. When I came home late, the broom and dust pan were out of their normal place and were propped by the back door. When I looked in the trash I not only found a broken glass bowl we used for fruit, but stacks of napkins with blood on them. At the time, I assumed someone had been cut when they broke the bowl or tried to clean it up.*

*The next day my mom had a black eye and her nose was swollen. I didn't see it until that night when I went to check on her. She'd been in bed all day.*

*"Oh, my God, mom."*

*"I was mopping the floor and had the fruit bowl in my hand and I slipped and fell face first into the corner of the table."*

*"Are you okay? Do you need to go to the doctor? What if you have a concussion?"*

*Her no was fast and fierce. And then she smiled.*

*"I'm fine, honey."*

But that is all history. My dad is in prison for the next few years. They are officially divorced now. And we have a new life in California.

I push the note away. I grab a soda and an apple from the refrigerator and decide to go eat it on the back deck before I begin editing my current film project.

I step out onto the deck and stretch. I still have to pinch myself that I live in California in a house on the beach. Well, at least until my mom finds a better job and we move out. But Oscar insists he loves the company. I don't think he has a boyfriend or anything so I can get that he might be a little lonely.

The beach in front of me is busy. Several people are sunbathing on towels and blankets. Others jog or stroll by. A few splash in the surf. We are a little bit north of the more popular stretch of beach so we don't always have people right in front of the house. But it's such a gorgeous day the entire long stretch of beach is dotted with people.

I stand there leaning my elbows on the rail and eating my apple when I see somebody on the beach staring at me. I jump.

It's Dylan. He has a gigantic smile on his face. I can feel my face grow hot. He waves. I wave back What the hell?

He waves for me to come down.

I only hesitate for a minute. I'll tell him I have to study and can't really talk long.

It's only partly true. It's mostly because he's forbidden. He's the boy I would be with in another life. And he knows it.

A few second later I'm coming across the sand toward him. He smiles as I grow closer and I think about how he really is hot. And not a bad kisser, either.

As soon as I think this I feel guilty and can my feel my face grow even redder with heat.

"Hey," I say, as soon as I'm close.

"Hey, yourself."

"Are you stalking me?" I say it in a joking voice, but I'm halfway serious.

"I guess I have to. You didn't answer my Snap."

I shrug.

He points down the beach. "See that stage?"

I look. There is a stage set up on the beach.

"Yep."

"We're filming a music video there today.

I'd heard some music when I first pulled up to the house a while ago.

"We're on a break," he says. "I remember you said you lived here. That's why I was Snapping you. I thought maybe we could have lunch while I'm in the area...I was just walking down the beach wondering which house was yours and as luck would have it, you were actually standing out on the deck."

"As luck would have it."

"What were the odds?" he says.

"Honestly? Not great. I rarely come outside when the beach is crowded like this."

"Wow. So, the stars aligned."

I don't answer.

"Want to walk down and say hi to the band?" It's hard to hear him. The waves are crashing loudly, people are talking and the wind has picked up.

"I can't," I say. I look down at the sand. The wind is blowing my hair everywhere.

"Just as a friend?"

"I don't think it's a good idea."

He leans in close to me. "I can barely hear you," he says.

His face is so close. Close enough to kiss. He looks me in the eyes and I can tell he's thinking the same thing. I close my eyes and bite my lip. I have to get out of here. He reaches over and gently tucks a wisp of hair that's blowing madly in the wind behind my ear. His touch sends a thrill of desire through me.

"Dylan?" I say in a pleading voice.

He pulls his head back. He turns and faces the water. I do, too. We stand side by side. He reaches out and squeezes my hand. I squeeze back but then draw my hand away and hug myself.

"You know how I know that I really like you and not just like you because I can't have you?" he says.

I make a face. "Oh, brother. Let's hear it."

He laughs. "It's because when you really care about them you want them to be happy no matter what, right? And I'm going to put myself out here right now and say that that's never really happened to me before. When I want someone and they don't want me I usually want them to be miserable. But with you I want you to be happy even if it's not with me. That has to mean something, right?"

I shrug. I'm getting super uncomfortable.

He must sense it because he says, "I'm not like a normal dude who just grunts and pretends they don't feel and think these things. I think that's why I'm a songwriter. I got a lot of emotions and I don't mind sharing them. I'm sorry if this is too much for you."

"It's different," I admit.

Then he turns. "You know what makes you irresistible?"

I laugh, embarrassed. I just shake my head.

"You are such a good girlfriend."

I don't answer.

"Like when you reject me, do you know what I think? I think she would be the perfect girlfriend for me because this douche bag boy band singer will not let up on her and she is so damn loyal to her boyfriend even though she's totally attracted to said douche bag."

I turn to leave. He reaches for my hand. "I'm sorry, I went too far."

I stare stonily at him. "Yeah, you did."

He lets go of my hand and looks down at the sand.

I turn and walk back toward the house. There's nothing else to say.

As I'm walking back, I see a flash of something at the neighbor's house that catches my eye. That woman was probably spying on me and is going to tell my mom everything. Weirdo.

## 17

Before I'm inside the house, my phone dings. It's a text from Dylan. I know I shouldn't but I open it.

"You can't be angry at me for telling the truth. Because whether you want to admit it to yourself or not, there's something there between us. Call it attraction or whatever you want, but you cannot look me in the face and deny it, Kennedy."

I don't respond.

I spend the night editing at the kitchen counter, leaning over my laptop and trying to get everything just right.

Oscar and my mom keep forcing food my way and telling me to go to bed.

Hunter texts me "I miss you. I want to see you. Tomorrow?"

It makes me smile.

I set my phone down on the counter and keep working.

Finally, I can't keep my eyes open any longer and stumble upstairs and crawl into bed.

When I wake in the morning, I hear voices downstairs

Fuck. Can't that woman stay in her own damn house? I think. I know I'm crabby and that I shouldn't begrudge my mom a new friendship. But coffee every morning?

Ugh.

My phone is right beside her. I was wondering where I'd left it. When I woke, I couldn't find it.

I walk over and scoop it up. There's a text from Hunter. He is asking if he can pick me up tonight after his AA meeting. I smile.

I even say good morning to Samantha. My mom smiles when I do. I feel guilty and vow to be politer to Samantha from here on out. She can't help it she's such a pest. She's just lonely, I know.

That night, I'm ready when Hunter pulls up and run out. He jumps out of the Jeep and gives me a big hug. His smile is the best thing ever. Then he grabs me and kisses me, pressing me up against the hood of the Jeep. His head bends to kiss my neck and I see something at the neighbor's house—a curtain close. I jump.

"Jesus Christ!"

"What, Boots?" He draws back with an alarmed look.

"The neighbor."

"Huh?" He turns to where I am pointing.

"This woman moved in next door. She's friends with my mom and she's always creeping. I've caught her spying on me a bunch lately. She doesn't really leave her house and it seems like she's all in our business about everything. It's gross."

He frowns and scowls in the direction of the house. "That's weird. Do you think maybe she's just lonely?"

I shrug.

"Maybe it's that," he says. "I doubt she means anything by it."

"She can fuck off," I say. Even I'm surprised by the vehemence in my voice.

"Oh, be nice, Kennedy," Hunter says.

Those words make me lose my mind.

"Don't ever tell me to be nice. Nice is for idiots. Nice is for people who get taken advantage of. Nice is for fools."

He stares at my outburst for a minute. I'm expecting him to argue back. Instead, he just shrugs.

"Whatever. Be mean, then." He opens his eyes wide and gets the desired effect because I burst out laughing.

"Fine. I am mean."

"Whatever you are, you're all mine. Now get in, I'm starved."

We pull out of the driveway and he gives me a sideways glance. "I'm really craving pizza."

"Then let's get pizza."

"I mean I'm craving really good pizza. Pizza from a place that only a true New Yorker would know about."

"Nice try," I say without looking.

"Come on, Kennedy," he says and thumps the steering wheel. "I've been thinking about that place all day long. I only want that pizza."

"Here's the turn off for Jack's," I say with a sweet smile.

"You are mean."

"Told you."

We are digging into your slices of pizza while Hunter talks about all his new friends and how cool they are. How they have private jets and fly off to Europe for the weekends and this crazy life that is so foreign to us.

"Can you imagine?" he says. "Let's go to Paris for the weekend? What the fuck?"

I give a weak smile. I want so hard to be supportive of him and his new friends because all of this is so good for him. But I'm jealous. It's a cold, hard, embarrassing fact.

"Jake is really cool. Like you wouldn't even know that his dad just won an Oscar for best actor. I like that. He just seems like everybody else. You have to meet him someday, Kennedy. You'd love him. He's just sooo chill."

"Cool," I say.

If Hunter notices I have very little to say, he ignores it.

"It's weird, I just feel like a real bond with these guys. I mean we share so much personal stuff that it makes us close right away. I think it's just what I need. Like I said, knowing there are other really cool people who don't drink or use is really good for me," he says.

"I'm so glad," I say. And right then I do mean it.

When you love someone you want what's best for them, right? That's true love.

As soon as I think it, I'm suffused with guilt. Dylan told me almost that say thing. Damn him. He needs to get out of my head. Especially when I'm with Hunter.

I reach for Hunter's hand. "Wanna go make out at the beach?"

He throws down his half-eaten slice of pizza, stands and is halfway out the door, jiggling his keys. I'm laughing and right behind him.

## 18

Coral has been avoiding me since the night of the fight.

Dex is back at school but I still haven't seen him in the halls or at lunch.

Hunter says that it doesn't look like Josh is going to be punished for what he did. It sounds like there isn't enough evidence to say for sure he was the one kicking Dex. It was too dark. It's so unfair. Josh seems like he has a golden shield around him, allowing him to do all his illegal and dickish stuff and never get caught or have to face any consequence.

Today, I sit with Paige and Emma in the cafeteria at lunch. Devin is sitting with some other guys. I don't know where Dex is.

I take a bite of my cheese stick and decide how I can ask about Coral. After I chew and swallow, I decide just to be blunt.

"Does Coral hate me? She won't return my messages."

Paige stares at me for a second and then shakes her head. "She doesn't hate you. Why don't you go to her softball game tonight?"

"That's a good idea."

Emma smiles. "I'd go with you but I have a date."

"Oh, my God. Spill it," I say.

We spend the rest of lunch talking about this shy senior who asked her to go get coffee after school.

"We've been facetiming and messaging," she says.

Of course, we make her show us pictures. "Oh, he is a fine-looking boy," Paige says.

We dork out over boys for a while and then Paige gets a smug smile. "There's someone I've been messaging, too. I don't know if it's anything, but he's pretty amazing. And you guys know him."

"What? You've been holding out?"

Emma leans over. "Tell us, bitch! We know him?"

Paige blushes and looks down.

"Come on!" I say.

She looks back up. "Remember when we met Sunset Patrol? I didn't really talk to him that night. He was sitting by you, Kennedy."

Suddenly, my face grows icy cold. My smile feels fake as fuck, but I try to maintain it.

"He's the lead singer," she says.

"Dylan?" Emma shouts with excitement.

I feel like I'm going to vomit. I've never told Paige or Emma about keeping in touch with Dylan. Mainly because Paige is Hunter's step-sister. I'm sick with jealousy and also fear. This is so, so bad. What if he tells her about us? I mean, there's nothing to tell except ... everything I didn't tell her. He kissed me. And I kissed him back. Hunter and I were broken up. But still.

Paige and Emma are talking excitedly about Dylan. How cute he is. How talented he is.

I swallow the icy fear and smile. "He remembers meeting us? What did he say?" I'm totally fishing to say if he mentioned me.

"Yeah, he says he thought we were really cool. He says they are filming part two of a music video on Pacific Beach tomorrow and said I should go."

"Oh, my God!" Emma is squealing. "He invited you to go see him? He likes you. For sure. You don't just invite anyone to that. Has he said he likes you? Like that you're cute or anything? DO you think he likes you that way?

I can't breathe as I wait for her answer.

She blushes again. "I don't know. I just snapped him out of the blue and he snapped me back. And then he was asking how I am. I asked if he remembered meeting us and he said of course."

"Oh," I say. Emma shoots me an odd glance. Fuck. I have to get my shit together.

Part of my heart is breaking for Paige and part of me is green with jealousy. After what happened with Paige and her college boyfriend, I am also surprised she's even considering hanging out with a guy again. She told me that she was strictly concentrating on school and her internship from here on out.

"What about your school and internship?" I say. I immediately feel guilty. Because my motives for asking are not pure. "Do you think he knows you have a crush on him?"

Paige frowns. "I don't know. I mean probably every girl in the universe likes him so I'm trying to play it cool, but Oh, my God. Dylan from Sunset Patrol is messaging me."

Emma squeals and holds her hand.

Just then the bell rings. I've never been so happy to go to my chemistry class.

## 19

After school, I head straight to the softball field.

Our team is warming up. I sit by myself in the bleachers. I can see when Coral notices me. She is leaning down tying her cleats when she must catch sight of me because her head jerks up and we meet eyes.

Then she looks away.

I smiled at her, but I think she looked away before she saw it.

"Hey stranger."

It's Dex and Devin. I jump up and hug them both. When I hug Dex I say, "I was so worried about you."

He gives me a goofy grin. "I'm good. Back to normal. Well, almost. I still have some fuzzy parts about what happened that night."

"I told him that he was doing a really cool trick on a skateboard, did a flip and everything and then hit his head."

Dex rolls his eyes. "I remember we were fighting with Josh and his dickhead friends, but that's about it."

I frown. "Do they think your memory is going to come back?"

I don't add what I'm thinking, *So you can tell the cops that it was Josh who did that to you.*

He nods. "Yeah," he says and knocks his fist on his head. "They say it's all in there. It will come back."

Just then Devin nudges us. "Coral's up to bat."

We grow quiet and all eyes focus on her walking up to home plate.

Coral sees us and blows Dex a kiss. He stands up. "Go Tangerine Girl! Knock it out of the park!"

She salutes him and then chokes up on the bat. I'm holding my breath watching as she swings and misses the first ball.

"Strike!" the umpire says.

"Shit," I mumble under my breath.

"You got this, girl!" Devin says.

"Go Tangerine Girl!" Dex says again.

Another ball flies past her as she swings with a whoosh.

"Strike two!"

Now we are all on our feet whistling and cheering encouragement.

The third ball is thrown and it's as if it's in slow motion as Coral swings and connects with a crack. I'm screaming and jumping and shouting as the ball flies over the small fence past center field. Dex and Devin and I are hugging each other and screaming when Coral strides across home plate with the grace of a panther.

"You are amazing!" I scream.

Then she looks up at me and smiles.

And I cry.

Dex and Devin sit down as the next batter comes to the plate. But I'm standing there, crying.

And as Coral walks to the dugout I see she is, too.

Devin pulls me down and puts his arm around me.

"It's okay. You know you guys love each other. Sometimes friends get mad at each other. It's okay."

I sniff and wipe my tears away with my sleeve.

When the game is over, Coral meets us right outside the ball field.

"Pizza on me?" I say.

She walks over and hugs me. "I missed you, girl," she says. "I'm sorry."

I hug her back. "I missed you, too. I'm sorry, too."

Then she pulls back. "Let's go. I worked up a ferocious appetite."

Dex slings his arm around her. "Damn right! You are a fucking phenomenon. Five home runs. Jesus! I'm so proud of you."

I am smiling so hard my face hurts.

We have so much fun at the pizza place. Especially when we walk in and the rest of the team is already there. They cheer when they see Coral. She's a star.

It seems like most of the school is at Jack's Pizza. It's loud and crazy and fun.

The four of us laugh and tell stories and I think that the only thing that could make this night more perfect is if Hunter was there.

And then, just like that, he walks in.

"Heard you guys were having too much fun without me."

I jump up and hug him. And then he hugs Dex and Devin and Coral. I love that Hunter and his friends hug each other. None of them are afraid to be affectionate like that.

Hunter and I hug and kiss so long that a group at another table starts hitting their forks on their glasses like people do when they want the bride and groom to kiss at a wedding reception. We burst into laughter.

Hunter devours what's left of our pizzas, drinks half the pitcher of soda and then excuses himself to go to the bathroom. We are starting to fade. After being excited and energetic all night the four of us are all yawning. We sit there and then Hunter's phone lights up with a notification. He's left it face up on the table next to me.

I glance down. It says Snap from @naughtynatalie. I frown at the name.

Coral gives me a look. I look away. What the fuck? Who calls themselves Naughty Natalie. I suddenly want to kill whoever that girl is.

Hunter comes out of the bathroom and is at the counter ordering something when the phone flashes again. This time it's just me and

Devin at the table. Dex and Coral have joined Hunter at the counter. Devin is on his phone. I glance down at Hunter's phone.

It's a text from a Natalie. "We missed you tonight. Tomorrow?"

The phone goes black right when I figure out who Natalie is. Or might be. That girl from the Palm Springs detox program.

I'd briefly noticed her when I went to visit him in Palm Springs. She was lying by the pool, but I just took her in with all the other young actresses in the program without thinking about it.

Then, the night he returned home, his dad threw a big party with a bunch of actors and film people. I had seen a picture of Hunter talking to a blonde girl and said I thought she looked vaguely familiar. When I asked him about it he said she was an actress his dad knew and that he'd become friends with her during detox. He told me that I had nothing to worry about.

I'd totally forgotten about her. Until now.

They came back empty handed. "I wanted to order another pizza but they said the kitchen's closed."

Dex yawned. "Yeah, we gotta bail anyway."

The three of them stood. Hunter remained sitting. "Can I just dust off the rest of this then?"

"All yours, hungry boy," Coral says.

"I'll wait with you," I say.

"I should hope so," Hunter says.

After the others have walked out. I tap his phone. "Your phone was lighting up. You got a couple messages."

He arches an eyebrow and reaches for his phone. "Oh, yeah?"

"Yeah," I say, watching his face closely. "From Natalie."

He frowns. Then he opens them and smiles. "Crap. I forgot to tell them I wasn't going to eat. Oh well."

He puts down the phone and turns to me. "I missed you so much. When Devin snapped that he was here and I saw you were, too, I drove like a hundred miles an hour to get here before you guys left."

I laugh and say, "You were just hungry." All my fears and jealousies and insecurities disappear at his words.

He leans over and kisses my neck. "I'm hungry for way more than pizza."

Then his phone lights up again. He picks it up and opens the snap. It's a very, very seductive picture of the blonde girl, Natalie. She's in a bed and she's leaning back with this look in her eyes. He instantly puts down the phone and looks at me.

"What the fuck?" I say.

"Kennedy," he says. "I swear I had no idea she was sending me a picture like that."

"What kind of pictures does she usually send?"

"Like ones of the group and stuff out eating. I swear."

All the jealousy I felt earlier is back and spills out of me. "When you said you had all these new friends in AA, you forgot to tell me that Natalie was one of them."

He looks down. And doesn't say anything.

"Hunter!?"

He looks up and is chewing his lip as he answers. "I was worried you'd get jealous."

"Well, fuck yeah, I'm jealous when I see a girl sending you pictures like that."

He meets my eyes. "Kennedy, I swear that's the first picture she's sent like that. I mean, do you think I would just open up a snap in front of you if I would've known that's what it was going to be? Think about it."

I exhale. I hate to admit it, but what he is saying makes sense.

The pizza place is empty now and the cashier is out from behind the counter stacking chairs on tabletops.

I stand. "Let's go. It's late."

When we are out at my car, I turn to him. "Hunter, I try really hard to not do anything or talk to anyone in a way that might make you jealous. Even if you aren't around or would never know. I just wish you would do the same."

"Hold up," he says. "You can't ask me not to talk her. That's not fair. You need to trust me. Remember we talked about that? Natalie is part of my friend group. It's really important that I have these friends. She's part of that."

He pauses. I don't respond so he keeps talking.

"These guys are keeping me clean and sober. I know you don't get it. It's hard for someone not in AA to understand."

That's when I lose it.

I back up. "I don't get it? I don't get it? But Natalie does? I'm the one who has cleaned up your puke numerous times. I'm the one who has put up with all your flaky shit when you're drinking. I'm the one who has spent a sleepless night in bed beside you to make sure you don't choke on your vomit. I'm the one who has stuck with you through all that, Hunter." I cross my arms. "So, don't you dare fucking tell me I don't get it."

His face falls. "I'm so sorry. That's not what I meant."

"Whatever." I'm steaming.

"Listen," he says, leaning down to look into my eyes. "I said that wrong. You get it. I didn't mean that. But I really get a lot of support from the other people in my group. And I don't think it's fair that you don't want me to talk to her. I swear Kennedy, we're just friends. I don't know what that picture was about. She has a boyfriend. I think she's just sort of like that. It doesn't mean anything. I swear. You have nothing to worry about. I promise."

I close my eyes for a few seconds. I believe him. I really do.

"Can we just talk about this tomorrow?"

He scowls. He stares at me for a few seconds. I just don't want to deal with it right now. I'm tired and emotional and afraid of what I might say.

He turns and gets into his Jeep, slamming the door behind him.

For a second I want to chase after him or call him and tell him to come back.

But I think I need to wait until tomorrow. By then I'll have calmed down.

Because I'm furious, but at the same time I realize my anger is at that girl named Natalie. What a bitch. Hunter is a fool for not realizing she's making a play for him. But I can see right through her. And I hate her with a passion.

## 20

The next day I'm busy with school and then spend most of the night doing homework and editing. It's only when I fall into bed close to midnight that I realize that Hunter has never texted me or messaged me. I also realize that I haven't had anything to eat since we had pizza.

I want to reach over and text him but it seems like so much effort. I can barely keep my eyes open.

The next thing I know it's morning.

I reach for my phone. Nothing from Hunter. Weird. In the back of my mind I think of that girl. Natalie. I push that thought down. We're good. I'm not clingy. He loves me.

I shoot him a snap. But I make sure it's sexy as hell. I wait until I'm out of the shower and I let my towel slip, just a little. But enough. *Take that, bitch*, I think as I send it to him.

But he doesn't answer.

Before I leave for school, I text him. "You okay? I haven't heard from you?

Now I'm really sick to my stomach. The thought of food makes me want to barf. I know it's my anxiety. Every time he's been flaky and gone off the grid, it's been because he's been drinking or doing drugs.

I think back to how we said goodbye, worried that something was said or done to trigger something making him drink, but I can't think of anything.

It's true that he seemed angry when I told him that I wanted to wait until the next day to talk about my anger and jealousy about his friendship with Natalie. But that can't possibly be reason enough to cause him to go drink or not respond to my snaps and messages.

I've just pulled the minivan into the parking lot at school when my phone explodes. I put the van in park and start pulling up texts and messages and snaps.

The first one is a text from a number I don't recognize. I open it and stare in shock at the picture that loads.

It's Hunter. With a blonde girl. They are holding hands and seem to be running away from a crowd of photographers with flashbulbs going off. The picture is from some tabloid. It has a caption, "Natalie Austin spotted at Hollywood Nightclub with sexy mystery man. Sources say he left longtime girlfriend to be with starlet."

Suddenly I can't breathe. I'm doubled over in pain, pressing my forehead on the steering wheel. My face feels icy cold. There is not enough air in the car. I want to throw open my door and run, screaming at the same time I want to curl up in the fetal position in my van. But I'm too paralyzed to do anything but stare at the van's dashboard.

Finally, when I catch my breath, I sit back up and start to read the messages and texts.

Coral: "What the fuck?"

Paige: "I swear I didn't know."

Emma: "I'm sorry. Where are you?"

Nothing from Hunter. Nothing.

I'm shaking as I open and read message after message.

A few Snap DM's from people I barely know. A few girls say random things, such as "You're way prettier than her" and "He's a jerk. You're better off without him."

Then the guys apparently feel the need to weigh in. I read them all, still feeling as if I'm in shock. Nothing seems real. A cute boy from my math class Snaps a DM: "He's a fool."

Another guy writes, "Oof. You're cute. Want to hang out." I don't even remember who he is and his bitmoji doesn't help me remember.

Then of course there are a few anonymous nasty ones.

One person writes that Hunter was smart to finally ditch my ugly ass and get with a girl who deserves him.

As soon as I read it, I know who wrote the next one: "I warned you, New Girl. Hunter only likes the bright new shiny things. You're old news, bitch. Welcome to the club."

Ava. She's so nasty. But I also can't stop thinking about what she said: "I'm not doing this for Josh." And that she wasn't in love with Hunter. There's more to that girl than meets the eye.

Then there is a message that surprises me. It's also anonymous. "You shouldn't be surprised. He left Carly for you. Of course, he's going to leave you for someone else. It's how it works."

I'm surprised to see Carly brought into this. And he was not with her when we met.

What I don't understand is how everyone knows that Hunter and I were supposedly still together when this photo was taken. Then I remember that most of the school saw us at the pizza place that night. And we were kissing and holding hands.

The other piece that makes me want to turn around and go home, is how my relationship with Hunter has not only become fodder for the tabloids, but something the entire school is talking about. What the hell?

What really stuns me is how did the paparazzi know that Hunter had a girlfriend? I frown. It's too neat a package. Somebody fed them the information. Suddenly, I know. That girl. She did. She told them he left me for her. It had to be her. Who else would know since they don't even know who Hunter is?

Finally, I've read every message and Snap. For some reason the torture of doing that seems like it put off the reality of the situation. But now I have to think about what that picture really means.

It's over.

~

IT DOESN'T TAKE LONG for the tabloids to figure out who Hunter is.

And he still hasn't texted me. Which makes me realize it's all true —there is no way what I saw in that picture is a mistake. I can try to justify it as much as I want, but the fact is he was out with Natalie Austin last night, holding her hand and not responding to my texts and messages.

I fight tears all morning. In my first three classes, people are looking at me and whispering. I remember what my dad taught me. I keep my head held high. It's not the first time I've been bullied at school, but earlier this year was the last time I let it get to me.

At one point, when I walk in to my AP Lit class and two girls I know shut up and stare at me, I walk over and stand directly in front them. "Is there something you want to say?"

They both grow red and shake their heads.

"I'm right here. If you have something to say about me, say it to my face," I say coolly.

One of them, Gretchen or something stammers, "Sorry."

I glare at her for a few seconds with my arms crossed over my chest. The other one starts to say something but I walk off. I don't care what lame ass excuse they have.

Even though I can't remember the last time I ate, I hide in the library at lunch. And even though I know it's a terrible idea, I log onto a laptop computer there. Now that I know her name, I search every mention of Natalie Austin.

All the top stories are about her and her mystery man.

TMZ has it. Everyone has it. I want to barf.

Then, as I read more about her, I figure out why it's such a big story.

Not only is she famous, she and her rock star boyfriend have been the tabloid darlings for the past two months. I'd had no idea. They are an "It" couple, and it seems as if every move they make is a tabloid story.

Over the past two months, since they met on a private island of a

Greek tycoon, they've had stormy fights in public and then equally provocative public make up sessions. There are pictures of Natalie sunbathing nude on beaches while he rubs oil on her naked back. Then there are pictures of them drinking in public. And reports of heavy drug use.

There are articles about her everywhere.

One article has this headline, "Natalie Austin's boyfriend begs her to check herself into rehab. He says drugs destroying his girlfriend."

There is a picture of her slumped over being held up by two bodyguard looking guys. Her dress, already cut to her belly button is gaping open so one of her boobs is almost hanging out all the way.

Then I find more. Shots of her in the Palm Springs detox resort where she met Hunter. A photographer had pretended to be a patient there and snuck in to take photos of her. Most are her by the pool or in the gym on the treadmill wearing a ball cap that says, "Baller."

I lean forward, scouring all the pictures for any sign of Hunter being around her, even a hand or sleeve in the corner of a photo. I don't find anything.

Then new stories pop up. The latest one is about Hunter:

"Natalie Austin's mystery man identified: son of director for her upcoming picture."

Then it gets crazier. Apparently, her rock star boyfriend found out about Natalie and Hunter and went berserk. He'd been arrested after he destroyed a hotel room at the Ritz Carlton in Paris.

A picture shows him leaving jail with his attorneys. I study his face. He is cute in an older guy way. He has long shaggy hair and full sensual lips. He wears leather pants and a white button down shirt with only one button done. A cigarette hangs out of the corner of his mouth.

I stare at him for a long time. He glares at the camera. I wish I could go destroy a hotel room. I feel like I could. But I'm stuck in my high school library feeling a mix of rage and betrayal and utter hope-lessness and sadness. I want to cry but for some strange reason I haven't yet.

I've also ignored all the texts from my girls. I know I'm in denial.

I glance at the time. I still have three more classes. But I don't have it in me to walk into the stares and whispers any more today. Once the bell rings and the halls clear of students, I grab my stuff and head for the parking lot. I still have three classes today but I can't do it I just can't.

I'm about to get into my car when I feel sick. I put my palm on my car door and try not to puke. But I do. It goes everywhere. I look around but nobody has seen me. Still feeling awful, I get in the van and drive home.

When I walked in, my mom and that bitchy neighbor from next door were on the deck in lounge chairs. I didn't want to talk to my mom in front of her so I hoped they didn't see me as I made my way to the stairs, but the neighbor turns and stares at me. I freeze. But she doesn't say anything. She just gives me a strange look and turns back around to talk to my mom.

I grab a bottled water and a handful of grapes on my way upstairs.

Upstairs, I crawl into bed.

When I wake, it's dark.

I'd fallen into bed on top of my covers but now there is a soft furry blanket from the couch downstairs. My mom must have come to check on me and covered me up. It makes me want to cry.

Then I remember. And I want to cry even harder, but there are no tears.

Instead, I throw up the water and grapes I just ate.

It's not the first time this has happened. The night my dad attacked my mom and nearly killed her, I hit him with a baseball bat. Then I sat there in the corner practically comatose until the emergency workers came to take them both to the hospital. I didn't cry that day. But I did barf a lot.

Two weeks later when my mom turned to me in her hospital bed and began to cry, that's when I bawled like a baby.

I wonder if I'm still in that weird state of shock. And over a boy. Stupid. It's not even a life or death thing. Just a broken heart. Happens every second of every day probably. I need to find out one thing and then I'm going to be over it. Over Hunter. He's broken my heart for the last time.

I know I'm going to regret it, but I grab my phone and send Hunter a one-word text:

"Why?"

He immediately replies, "You know why."

What the hell? I throw my phone down. I'm not going to play his stupid games.

But the pit in my stomach makes me bowl over and hold my gut.

Then I throw up again. But this time it's bile. I realize that one reason my stomach hurts is because I'm hungry. Starved, really. I haven't eaten for more than 24 hours. I get up and head downstairs to forage for food. All the lights are off except the one over the stove that Oscar keeps on all night. I wonder if my mom and Oscar know what happened? If they saw all the tabloids, too? Probably not. But someone might have told them. I remember the odd look our weirdo neighbor gave me when I snuck in the house.

I bet she knows. She's the kind of grown woman who would read tabloids. I bet she saw it and maybe told my mom. That's probably why my mom let me sleep.

I open the refrigerator and see what looks like some foil-wrapped slices of pizza on the bottom shelf. I reach down to grab it and for a second I feel dizzy and then everything goes black.

The next thing I know my mom is standing over me holding her cell phone.

"Hurry, please come," she says. "And then, oh my God, she opened her eyes."

I blink and start to sit up, but feel woozy. She cradles my head and puts it back. It's on a pillow.

"What?"

"You passed out honey. I called 911."

I struggle to sit up again. "I'm okay."

"They're already here. Let's just have them check you out, okay?" It's Oscar. His face looms far above me.

"I'm fine," I say. I really do feel better. Sort of. The room is spinning. I feel tingly.

Then the paramedics are taking my vitals. Asking my name. Asking the day and who the president is.

I'm lifted to a gurney.

"I'm fine, really," I say. But I don't feel fine. I feel weird still.

In the back of the ambulance, they give me an IV.

My mom sits beside me holding my hand. Her forehead is creased with worry.

"Can you die of a broken heart?" I say, and give a strangled laugh.

"What?" She half laughs.

"Guess you didn't hear about Hunter and his new movie star girlfriend?"

I can tell by the look on her face this is brand new to her. "Oh no. I'm so sorry."

Then she gives me a weird look and leans over, "You didn't take anything ... did you?"

I stare at her in shock. "Oh, my God! No! No! Mom! I would never do that."

She closes her eyes and exhales. She pats my hand and opens her eyes. "Okay. I didn't think so, but wanted to check. The paramedics had asked me."

"No!" I say again.

Whatever they got pumping in the IV is working. I'm starting to feel more like myself and irritated that I'm being taken to the hospital. At least the sirens aren't on.

My mom looks down at her phone and types something. I look at her suspiciously. "What?"

She exhales loudly. "I know it's none of my business. But your nice friend Emma had texted me saying she was worried about you. She wouldn't say why."

"Oh, no, Mom," I say. Fuck.

"I told her you were okay but we were having you checked out at the hospital just in case."

I practically sit up in dismay. "No! Mom! Shit! This has nothing to do with what she was asking about. Shit!"

"Kennedy. Language."

I'm sitting up now. "I don't care."

The paramedic is hovering over me. "Please lay back down. I can raise your bed up if you like."

I glare at my mom and put my head back down. Jesus.

"I'm sorry, Kennedy," my mom says in an indignant voice. "She reached out to me. I'm not going to ignore her. She only did because she was worried and she cares. I would never contact your friends on my own, but I'm sure as heck going to respond if they reach out to me."

I sigh. "I know. It's just..."

It's just fucked up.

At the hospital, my mom and I wait in a room for the doctor to come in. A nurse has taken all my vitals and a blood draw and now we just wait. I have messages from Emma and Coral.

I respond to all of them in a group text with a goofy photo of me in the hospital gown giving a peace sign. I write, "I passed out. My mom is overreacting."

Emma sends a heart. Coral sends praying hands. Nothing from Paige.

Thinking of her fills me with guilt. She likes Dylan and she doesn't know that he and I have been in touch for months. Platonically. Well, me pushing him away. But still.

Maybe he likes her now. I'd be happy for them both. It would sting a little. But we don't stand a chance. Dylan is hot and rich and funny and kind and would make an amazing boyfriend. But he pales compared to Hunter. He just does.

Then the doctor comes in and smiles. He's an older guy with thick glasses, a paunch, and a ready smile.

"Well, young lady, it looks like you were pretty badly dehydrated. Did you forget to eat and drink?"

I nod, guiltily. I don't mention it was partly from throwing up. Too embarrassing.

"Try not to do that again. It will save you a trip here."

I nod. "We've given you some electrolytes in your IV and your blood pressure seems back to normal. want to keep an eye on you for another hour but then I think you're good to go back home."

My mom sighs loudly. "Oh, thank God."

I shoot her a look. She was really worried.

"Sounds good," I say.

"Why don't you just relax and the nurse will be back with your discharge papers in about an hour if everything remains the same."

My mother thanks him. He dims the lights as he leaves. I lay back down and pull the thin hospital blanket over me, suddenly cold. For whatever reason, I'm sleepy again. Which is ridiculous since I slept all day. But I start to drift off and the hour passes quickly.

We get home about one in the morning and I hug my mom and turn toward the stairs to my room.

"Kennedy?" my mom says. "Oscar told me about the picture." She holds up her phone. "I'm sorry."

I nod.

The next morning, I can tell I've slept in past the first class by the light shining in my curtains. I don't care. I'm not going to school today. I need a mental health day. I grab my phone and stay in bed watching TikToks. Then as I'm holding my phone it rings, startling me. It's Hunter.

I am tempted to ignore it, but I hit answer but don't say anything.

"Can we talk?" he says.

"Fuck off," I say and hang up.

It feels good. At first. But then it hurts. Bad. I curl up into a ball and pull the covers over my head. I put in my earbuds and pull up a song list that usually makes me cry. But then at the last minute, I switch it to a song list I made to use when I used to go running. I crank it. It's angry and full of rage and it drowns out all my thoughts.

My phone dings. I ignore it. It dings again. And again.

"What?" I say and grab it. Hunter. "I'm out front."

I throw back my covers. The music has me enraged.

I've spend the past twenty-four hours vacillating between anger, sadness and numbness.

Right now, I'm back to pure fury.

I stalk out of my room. I catch a glimpse of myself in the hall mirror. My hair is tangled and dirty. I have black circles under my eyes since I never took my eye makeup off yesterday. I'm wearing giant flannel pajama pants and a shirt that says Queen. At least the shirt is suitable.

The rest of me looks homeless but the shirt says everything Hunter needs to know. I'm done. He doesn't deserve a girlfriend like me. I would never ever cheat on him.

I fling open the door and turn around and walk back into the house. After a few seconds, I hear him follow and the door close. I pull up a bar stool at the counter. There is a note from my mom. She's next door at the neighbor's working if I need her. She'll check on me at lunch. It's eleven. I hope she comes early so Hunter can explain to her, too, how he broke my heart.

I feel him beside me before I see him.

"You okay? Dex told me they took you to the hospital last night."

I shouldn't be surprised. Tell Coral something and Dex knows. If Dex knows, Hunter knows. It's basic math in our friend group.

I shoot him a dirty look. "Fine," I say. Then I turn to him. "If that's why you're here, because you think somehow that what happened to me last night had something to do with you, you're wrong. I was dehydrated and anemic. I'm not like your last girlfriend, Hunter. I don't need to hurt myself when you don't want me anymore."

He flinches. It's a verbal slap in the face and I don't care.

Every time Hunter tried to leave Carly, she would end up trying to hurt herself. It's actually heartbreaking when you really think about it. I'd feel sorrier for her if she hadn't handcuffed me, drugged me, and generally tried to ruin my life.

I put my hands on my hips and stare at him, willing him to talk. Finally, he does.

"I'm sorry about the picture. It all got out of hand really quickly."

I make a big show of yawning. "Hunter? If you're here to confess and relieve your conscience to make yourself feel better, spare it. I don't want to know. I don't need the details. You can just leave now."

His face is stone and he turns on the bar stool to face me and crosses his arms across his chest.

"You're the one who asked why." He raises an eyebrow as he says it.

I swallow and look down.

"Will you hear me out?"

I close my eyes for a second and open them. I do want to know why. If I know why, maybe I can move on instead of always wondering. I look up at him. "Yes."

"It was pure and utter retaliation," he says.

*I've been dating a child. I gave my heart to an immature bully bad boy who just crushed it and then stomped on it.*

He runs a hand through his hair. Then he jumps off the stool and I take several steps back. His eyes are black with fury. "I did it to get you back. I wanted you to feel the hurt that I feel. God damn it. How could you?"

He pounds his fist on the bar counter. The bowl of fruit and the salt and pepper shaker jump.

"What are you talking about?" I can feel my whole face scrunched up in confusion. "What? Don't blame this on me."

He's mad because I got jealous of a text from that bitch actress and didn't want to talk about it right away? That's total bullshit. He gets mad at me in return and then goes and cheats on me and says it's my fault.

He's crazy.

He shoots me a look I can't read. But then he keeps talking.

"I walked into that meeting and I," he looks down and shakes his head. "I shared what I was feeling and going through. You got to understand. That's what we do. Instead of me going and getting drunk or high, I talk to them and they talk me off the ledge."

I'm frowning. I hate that all these strangers, including that conniving blonde bitch, know our business, but if he says it keeps him from using or drinking ...

He's still talking. After the meeting, Natalie came up to me and said that she was sorry about what I was going through. Her boyfriend flew to Paris at the last minute for something and so she didn't have a date to some celebrity club opening and asked I wanted to come with her. She said it might cheer me up."

"I bet she did," I say and glare.

"It wasn't like that," he says and looks down. "At first."

My heart skips a beat. It feels like it's being squeezed. At first.

"At some point," he says. "I was so mad at you that I just leaned over and kissed her."

He pauses. I can't look at him. I stare at the floor.

"Kennedy?"

I shake my head. I'm afraid if I speak I'll cry.

"I wanted to hurt you. But not the way it happened. I didn't know the paparazzi were going to be waiting for us when we left. They chased us. For blocks. It was crazy. I've never been around that before. People screaming and chasing us and calling Natalie's name..."

I lift my head to meet his eyes coldly. He gets the hint and shuts up.

"And things had gone so well when you kissed her that you were holding her hand?"

He nods and exhales. "Yeah. But also, because we were running."

I shake my head. I'm disgusted by his entire story.

"I'm sorry but when I saw the texts and pictures and then Paige confirmed it, I just went a little crazy. I mean Jesus, Kennedy, if you wanted him, why didn't you just tell me and break up with me. I never thought you would cheat on me. I never thought you could do that to me."

I feel an icy chill run down my body. Texts. Pictures. Paige.

"Hunter?" I say. "I don't know what you are talking about. I mean it."

He frowns and looks at me.

We stare at each other for a few seconds and then he reaches into his back pocket for his phone. He taps it and then hands it to me.

I gasp at what I see. It's a photo of Dylan and me on the beach. He has his hand up and is brushing my hair back. Then there is one of him leaning in close to me.

That day on the beach. When he wanted me to go for a walk with him and I refused.

I look up at Hunter. "He came here. He was out on the beach. I went to talk to him. He wanted me to go for a walk with him. I told him I couldn't because I had a boyfriend and I didn't want to do anything that would make him—you—jealous."

Hunter just shakes his head. "Paige told me."

"Told you what?" My tone is icy cool.

He sighs. "Don't fucking lie to me. I went to Paige to ask her if she knew anything and she texted Dylan. He says he's madly in love with you."

I sputter. I have no words. I don't even know where to start.

"There's nothing between us. I swear."

He yanks the phone out of my hand. "Then explain these," he says and taps his phone and hands it back to me. It's a screen shot of a text from Dylan:

*"You can't be angry at me for telling the truth. Because whether you want to admit it to yourself or not, there's something there between us. Call it attraction or whatever you want, but you cannot look me in the face and deny it, Kennedy."*

I shake my head. Who would do this? Who would take these pictures and be able to get a screen shot of the texts on my phone? I think back to the day that Dylan stopped by. There were a lot of people on the beach that day who could have taken our picture. But the angle was a little bit high. A little above us.

"It's pretty fucking obvious to me," Hunter says and turns to leave. "You wanted to know why. That's why. I'm not proud of how I handled it. But I don't really care right now. You fucked me over. I'm glad you're okay. I was worried when I heard you were in the hospital. I don't hate you, Kennedy. I wish I could. But I don't think you should ever contact me again."

As he's been saying all this, my mind has been racing.

Then it all falls into place.

Samantha. Our neighbor. My mouth opens in horror. Because then I also remember how I'd left my phone on the counter overnight and when I got up, she'd been sitting by it.

"I don't understand," I say to myself in a low voice.

Hunter is at the front door. "Wait!" I shout. He doesn't stop.

"We've been set up!" I yell. He stops with his hand on the door-knob and his back to me.

## 21

Hunter squirms as we wait for someone to answer my knock at the house next door.

"I don't know what this is all about," he says.

"Me, either," I say. "But I swear I never cheated on you. The texts are real. The photos are real. But that's all there was to it. Not a damn thing more. Do you believe me?"

He makes a face. "I don't know."

Just come with me please," I say.

Now, he looks at me. "Why would some woman do this?"

"I don't know," I say. "But I'm going to find out."

The door opens and I'm ready to launch into a tirade, but it's my mom.

"Hi, honey," she says. Then she sees Hunter and raises an eyebrow.

"Mom, this is kind of weird but I need to speak to Samantha."

Her eyebrows draw together. "When the doorbell rang, she excused herself saying she wasn't feeling well. She asked me to handle whomever was at the door."

"Did she see it was me? And Hunter?" I ask.

My mom pauses for a second and then says, "Well, actually I

think she did. And she seemed sort of upset. Kennedy, what is all this about."

I walk past my mom inside. Hunter trails behind me. My mom stands with her hand on the doorknob staring at us.

It's the first time I've been inside the house. It's oddly sparse and empty. There is a couch, end table and a dining room table with chairs and that's about it. It's probably a multi-million-dollar home furnished with what appears to be furniture from Ikea.

"I don't know if you should be inside," she says. "I mean this is my bosses' house. I work for Samantha now, you know."

"Probably not after you hear what she did," I say.

My mom closes the door behind her. I see her shoulders square back. She meets my eyes. She must believe me because then she says, "I'll go get her."

I hear voices and arguing and then a door slam. My mom yells something. I look at Hunter and raise an eyebrow. Wow. My mom is usually very non-confrontational. She comes out and grabs her bag and sweater and starts toward the door.

"I'm sorry, Kennedy, she won't come out."

I stand in the entry way to the hall. "I'm not leaving until you come out. If you want I'll call the police and you can explain it all to them."

I hear a door open.

I back off and go stand by my mom, grabbing her hand.

Just then Hunter walks away from us toward a small table with a few framed photos.

Hunter has picked up a photo and I hear him swear loudly right when Samantha walks in. Then he turns quickly, looks over at Samantha, and his face grows white.

"Hunter," she says with a tight smile.

"What the fuck are you doing here?" Hunter says and his voice is full of rage.

## 22

Hunter turns to me and grabs my hand. "Let's get out of here before I kill her."

"What?"

I'm completely lost.

My mom is staring at us all, looking from me to Samantha to Hunter.

"Hunter? I don't get it," I say.

Samantha strides over to the small table with the photos and reaches for a bottle with something amber in it. She pours some of it into a short crystal glass and then tips it back, drinking the whole thing in one gulp.

"Why don't you explain?" Hunter says, his eyes narrowed as he glares at Samantha. "If you don't start talking I'm going to do exactly what Kennedy said and call the police."

She just laughs and pours yet another drink, saying, "Oh, Hunter, you're so dramatic."

After downing the second glass, she turns to us and her eyes grow cold. "Let's make this perfectly clear. You came into my house. You are accusing me of things that you cannot proof."

She lights a cigarette and blows it our way. "In fact, I could probably sue you for slander if you keep talking. Do you want to keep talking, Hunter?" she asks coolly.

## 23

M y mom takes charge.

"Don't you dare talk to my daughter or her boyfriend that way!" she says and walks over to Samantha. My mom yanks the cigarette out of Samantha's mouth and then slaps her across the face.

I'm stunned. Absolutely astonished.

Samantha holds her cheek with wide eyes.

"How dare you?" My mother says. "How dare you use me in this way. How dare you come after my daughter."

"Relax, Justine," Samantha says and looks down on her from her long pointy nose.

I'm over in front of Samantha in a second. "Don't you tell my mother to relax!" I shout.

My mom grabs my arm. "I've got this, Kennedy."

Her icy tone makes me back up.

Now my mom is standing inches away from Samantha's face.

"I want you gone," my mother says and lifts her finger to point toward the road. "If you are not packed and moved out of this house by tomorrow at sunrise, I will go to the police and share everything that has happened."

"You don't have the guts," Samantha says and glares at my mother.

My mother laughs. A mean laugh I've never heard before.

"Just try me."

Samantha's face clouds over. She leans over and her hand is shaking as she lights another cigarette.

"I'm dead serious," my mom says, glaring at Samantha. "Sunrise."

And then my mother turns, takes my arm, and storms out. We pass Hunter. He is staring at us both wide-eyed, but then springs into action, rushing to open the front door for us.

The three of us don't say a word until we are back in Oscar's house.

My mom sinks onto the sofa. I slump beside her. We look at each other and start to laugh. Soon we are cackling madly.

"That bitch!" my mother says.

Hunter has been standing at the bar counter the entire time. We hear car doors slam and he rushes to the front door.

Then he comes back with a triumphant smile. "I think she's gone."

I high five my mom.

But then I frown. "Wouldn't she need more than one car?"

My mom shakes her head. "No, she only had a suitcase or two. I should've known that was a red flag. The house was partially furnished. I can't believe that monster moved in next door just to mess with you, Kennedy. I'm so sorry that I fell for it."

I shake my head. "It's not your fault, mom. Anyone would've done the same."

She smiles at me, but then her smile fades.

"Do you think we should call the police anyway?" she says

I scowl. "I don't know."

"Me, either," she says. "I'm not sure if what she did was actually illegal."

Hunter has been sitting quietly at the bar. He stands. "I think I better go."

"I'll walk you out," I say.

In the driveway, we lean against his Jeep.

"Wow," he says. "Your mom was something else."

I nod. It was weird. But good. She never stood up for herself much when it came to my dad and his abuse. This was a new, different side of her. I was proud of her for standing up to that woman.

Then we both sit there quietly. It's awkward. Even though we were set up and manipulated and played, the whole thing really created some ugly feelings between us.

I swallow. "It feels kind of weird right now, doesn't it?"

He nods. He looks down at his boots.

I reach for his hand and squeeze it. "Want to just sleep on it and talk tomorrow? It's been a long day?"

He nods. He climbs into his Jeep without kissing me goodbye. It stings.

I wonder if Carly's mother got her way after all.

## 24

The next day, I text Paige as soon as I get to school.

"Can we talk."

She doesn't respond. I'm crushed. We've had misunderstandings before. I thought we were past all that. It makes me sad all day.

At lunch, I walk into the cafeteria by myself. I'd thought that Coral and Emma and Paige would be there. I mean, they usually text me if they are going out to eat. My heart sinks. What if they are all angry with me? My heart is heavy as I turn to walk out, my appetite gone.

As I do, I see them all walking in, laughing. Coral and Emma smile at me. Paige just stares. I walk right up to them.

"Can we talk in the hall for a minute?"

Paige looks like she's going to cry. She follows me out.

"When you first told me that Dylan was texting you I should've said something. I'm sorry. He's been in touch with me a few times since that night in Hollywood."

Her face is stony. "You kissed him, Kennedy."

I exhale loudly and nod. "I did. When Hunter and I broke up. But

I always told him that Hunter was my boyfriend and the one for me. He..."

"He's in love with you," Paige interrupts.

I nod meekly.

"It's just not fair," she says with passion. "I thought I'd finally met someone who could help me get over Greg. And it turns out he just was nice to me because I'm your friend."

"I'm sorry," I say. I feel like shit.

"It's fine," she says. But I can tell it's not.

"I would never ever hurt you, Paige. You have to believe me."

"I do," she says.

We stare at each other for a few seconds. And then, inexplicably I start to bawl. Tears are running down my face and snot is everywhere, I know.

"Kennedy!" Paige says in alarm.

I'm crying so hard I can barely speak. "I don't want anything to change. I don't want you to go away to college. You are such a good friend to me. I would never hurt you. I swear, Paige. I swear."

Then she is hugging me and I'm getting snot and tears all over her shirt.

She pulls back. "It's okay. It really is."

"You sure?" I say, sniffling and wiping my face on my sleeve.

"Yes," she says and smiles. "You're going to have to work a whole lot harder to get rid of me than that."

I smile at her gratefully.

We walk back into the cafeteria together and across the room I see Emma and Coral stop talking and look up at us. The smile they give us makes me start crying again.

# 25

The sun beats down on my skin and I know I could never move back to Brooklyn. It's only late April but there's been a heat wave and we are soaking up the heat and sun while it lasts.

The beach is packed. We all met at my house and are in the sand in front of our place. Oscar is on the back deck grilling hot dogs and hamburgers for our lunch. It smells great.

Hunter reaches over and lightly trails his fingers across my belly. I roll over onto my stomach and lift my sunglasses to look at him. He gives me a wicked grin. He knows that the slightest touch sets my body on fire.

I sit up and take in the sight of my friends surrounding me. Hunter is on one side of me. He has laid back down and I can see by his long lashes that he's closed his eyes again behind his sunglasses. Seeing his lean, bronzed body almost takes my breath away after all these months.

Paige is on the other side of me. She is reading a book. That girl is always studying. I don't know what she's going to do yet for a career, but whatever she decides, she's going to kill it. She looks at me over the pages of the book and winks.

Emma is on her stomach on the other side of Paige. She looks like she might be asleep. Devin is sitting up looking at the ocean. I catch him looking down at Emma and I raise an eyebrow. He makes a face and blushes. I know he started seeing some girl he works with at the café where he has started waiting tables.

On the other side of Hunter, Coral and Dex are curled up on a giant towel. They are talking softly to each other and giggling, lost in their own world.

These are my best friends in the whole world. Well besides Sherie back in Brooklyn. She will always be my best best even if we don't talk much anymore.

I try to memorize this scene. I close my eyes and try to imprint it on my memory. I know that this moment, this slice of my golden life, is fleeting. I wish I had my camera to film it. I realize that's why I want to be a director. I want to capture these moments, to create them for others so they feel this bittersweet surge of sheer joy that I feel right now.

Thinking of my camera makes me feel a little guilty. I've been phoning it in the past few weeks. Miss Flora, the film teacher, would never say anything, but the mini projects I've turned in haven't been my best work. I have another month to really focus on my final project. I vow right now to do it no matter what.

Then I turn my body toward the water, hugging my knees, and staring out at the vast sea that seems to stretch before me into infinity. I don't know how I landed here on this beach surrounded by these friends, but I know enough to realize that this is a moment I will remember forever. With or without my video camera.

## 26

I am wearing a new sundress that makes me feel mature and sophisticated. It has a square neck and is white linen. It's a deviation from my all black clothing. My mom bought me gold sandals with a small heel to go with it. I've pulled my dark hair back from my face the way Hunter likes it.

I can't wait for Hunter to show up. At the same time, I'm absolutely sick.

The deadline for him to respond about the Fulbright Scholarship is today. I want to ask him tonight if he's decided to go. But I just want to put off the answer for another few hours. I want to live in the ignorant bliss of not knowing.

As I wait for him to arrive, my mom sees my tapping foot and laughs.

"He'll be here any minute."

"I know."

She gives me a mysterious look. "What?" I ask.

"Oh, nothing." But her smile is giant. She's hiding something.

I smile myself thinking of the surprise I have for him. He thinks we are going to a fancy dinner. I told him to dress nice. Thinking about where we are going, I suddenly question my white dress. Pizza sauce doesn't look good on a white dress. Probably not a smart choice. Oh, screw it. It will be fine.

Then I hear his Jeep. I reach the door right when he knocks.

When I open the door, and see him, he takes my breath away.

He is wearing black pants, shoes, and a blazer. He has a tight navy T-shirt under his blazer that matches his eyes.

"Wow," he says when he sees me.

I blush.

He gives me a slow smile and I melt.

"Bye mom," I say and close the door behind us.

"Okay, then," he says and yells over my shoulder. "Nice to see you, too, Ms. Conner."

"Ha ha."

"You driving, right?" he asks.

"Yes." I give him a look. I'd already told him that earlier.

"Gonna tell me where we're going yet?"

"No way."

We head up the coast and then turn inland after about ten minutes. It's not a fancy area. It's more of a working-class neighborhood we are driving in. Hunter looks over at me and smiles.

"Are you?"

"Shut up!" I say interrupting.

Then the sign is before us: Marino's Pizza. It's lit up with flashing lights and in the Italian colors of red, green, and white.

"Yes!" Hunter says and thrusts his fist up in the air.

"You're not disappointed, are you?" I ask as we pull into the parking lot.

"You're joking, right?" he says.

"I mean if you were expecting a fancy restaurant..." I say and trail off.

"I'll take this place any day," he says.

We order a large pizza and Hunter eats most of it. I stare at him in awe.

"Dude," I say.

"I know," he says.

The Fulbright Scholar thing hangs in the air between us, but I don't want to ruin this night. I know eventually I'll have to ask if what he's decided, but I want to put it off as long as possible.

Then he walks up to the counter and orders another one to go.

"We need cold pizza in the morning."

"We do?"

He smiles. "You're not the only one with surprises."

"Oh, yeah?"

"We're driving to Santa Barbara for the weekend."

"Get out!" I say.

He grins. "Your mom is in on it. There's a suitcase she packed for you in the back of the van."

"Hold up," I say. "My mom thinks it's okay if we go off for the weekend together?"

He nodded and smiled. "I guess she likes me."

"I guess," I say.

I'm so excited. A weekend away with Hunter.

We walk out to the minivan and I peek in the very back. Sure enough there is a suitcase. Sneaky.

Then it hits me. "Wait? Isn't this weekend the Santa Barbara Film Festival."

He looks at me and the grin he gives me makes me scream.

"No!"

"Yes!"

"Spill it, Hunter!"

"We got an honorable mention. They are screening our film at the festival."

"Holy shit!"

"Your mom and Oscar rented a house for all of us, but they agreed I could surprise you and we would drive separately."

I scream again. "They are showing our film? For real?"

"Yep," he says.

"Oh. My. God," I say. "Wait. Miss Flora didn't say anything to me."

"She didn't know. The festival emailed me directly."

The drive to Santa Barbara goes quickly as Hunter and I talk about the festival and who might be there and what kind of exposure this screening could give us.

All of a sudden, I freeze. "I need a dress!" I shout.

"Oscar handled it."

I sink back down into my seat with relief. Whatever it is will be perfect. Oscar has impeccable taste.

When we get to the house in Santa Barbara they've rented, my mom and Oscar are already in bed in their rooms. Hunter said they hit the road as soon as we left for the pizza place so they could have the house ready.

There is a note on the table saying that our rooms are on the second floor. I laugh. I should've known better than to think my mom would have me and Hunter share a room. When we get upstairs, I stop at one bedroom and whisper to Hunter, "Looks like this is good-night then."

He follows me in and shuts and locks the door.

"Hunter! My mom!"

But when he kisses me, I'm the one who ends up tugging his shirt off and leading him to my bed.

I'd love nothing more than to fall asleep in his arms, but I make sure that he goes and sleeps in his own bed, though. Out of respect for my mom. If she wants us to have separate rooms we will do so.

The next day we tour Old Santa Barbara and take pictures at the Mission and have a really late lunch on the pier before we go back to the house and relax before the screening.

When I unpacked the suitcase that morning, I didn't see anything that would qualify as a suitable dress until I opened the closet to hang up a shirt and saw a stunning red strapless dress. I tugged it on and then stared at myself in the floor-length mirror. It fell to my ankles and hugged every curve. I didn't look like a teenage girl. I looked like a young woman. I stared at my reflection and wondered who this woman was. She was me and yet, not me.

When I walk out in the dress shortly before it's time to leave, Hunter clutches his chest. "Jesus, Kennedy. I don't think I can fight off all the guys who are going to hit on you tonight. Are you sure you want to wear that?"

I laugh. "Blame Oscar."

"Dude," Hunter says. "You trying to kill me or what?"

Oscar comes over and kisses my cheek. "You are exquisite."

"Thanks," I say and look at my mom. "Oh, my God, you are stunning, mom."

She is dressed in a silver sheath and her long hair is curled. Her skin glows and she has on the highest heels I've ever seen her wear.

"She's right," Hunter says. "You look beautiful."

My mom's face turns red.

Oscar taps his watch and tells us it's time to go.

He hired a limousine to take us to the old-fashioned theater where the film is showing. I feel like a movie star when we get out and step onto the red carpet leading into the theater. There are several photographers taking photos and I am temporarily blinded by the flashbulbs. It seems so unreal.

We are escorted to our seats in the theater and before long the theater darkens and the first of three films begin. Ours is the last one. By the time it shows, I'm nearly sick with anxiety and anticipation.

Our short romance is met with laughter and cheers. I watch in amazement that something I created is showing on a big screen. I look around the audience and when they react and laugh at the right moments. I can't stop grinning. It is utterly amazing.

Then, at the end, before the credits roll, there is a segment that I haven't seen yet. Miss Flora interviewed us and then edited the interviews to provide short outtakes at the end. I'm a nervous wreck waiting to see what she used.

Hunter's interview is first. His face so big on that screen makes me wonder how such a beautiful boy ever fell for me. But I also know he's so much more than his good looks.

The light from a window covers half his face making his words feel like a confession.

He talks about how he'd given up on love until his senior year. I'm stunned he is talking publicly about such a personal topic. And impressed.

"I had some things happen to me when I was growing up that made me hard," he says with a serious expression. "It's weird because I didn't even realize it. I didn't know I was hard until I met someone who made me soft. Love is not perfect. But when you meet someone who teaches you to love, you want to shout that from the rooftops. I know that's cliché, but it really does make me want to direct romantic dramas."

I have tears running down my face in the dark. Hunter leans over and kisses my cheek.

Then the screen shows my gigantic head. I lean back in my seat feeling awkward. My mom reaches over and puts her arm around me. My eyes are glued to the screen. And what is that horrid screech. Oh, my voice.

"A year ago," my face on the big screen begins. "I was broken. My future seemed bleak. But there was always one thing that could cheer me up even on my darkest days: the movie theater. At first, the thought of doing documentaries seemed depressing. I mean, I loved movies because they gave me an escape from all the crap in my real world. But going through all the things I did growing up, also gave me compassion. Now, when I come across someone having a bad day or being rude, I think that they might be having a rough time. But the stories that interest me the most are the ones that show ordinary people overcoming tremendous odds. That's what I'm hoping to focus on during my film career."

Then the screen goes black.

The audience erupts in whistles and cheers and applause.

An hour later, we all file into the massive penthouse restaurant with views of the ocean. The entire room is lit with candles. It feels like I've stepped into a fairytale. I'm surrounded by faces and names I've only read about. And they are congratulating me and Hunter, giving us business cards, and smiling at us. It's surreal.

My mom and Oscar bowed out of the party saying they were going back to the house to eat popcorn and watch Saturday Night

Live. I think they just wanted to give me and Hunter time alone to celebrate.

But Hunter's dad and stepmom must not have the same idea. They walk in and immediately Paige's mom catches my eye. They head our way. Mrs. West is wearing a floor-length dress and Mr. West has on a tux. They look like movie stars.

They head our way. I'm nervous. I know Hunter's dad doesn't like me. And I barely know Paige's mom even though the times we've met she's been super sweet.

Hunter let's go of my hand to go hug his dad who claps him on the back and says, "I'm proud of you son,"

I make small talk with Paige's mom.

"I just loved your film," she says.

Then I hear a throat clear and look up to see Mr. West in front of me.

"That was some damn fine filmmaking young lady," he says.

For some idiot reason, his words make tears spring to my eyes.

I hate myself that his words of approval mean so much. But I tell myself that along with being my boyfriend's dad, he's also a renowned director.

"I was talking to Oscar the other day. We hired him as the D.P. for our film this summer. He said that you might be interested in working on the set. I wasn't sure if I had a spot for you," he says.

My heart sinks. Of course, he doesn't.

But then he smiles. "But after seeing your work, I will make sure there is a spot for you on the set. I'd like to take you under my wing at least two days a week. I think you have a natural talent for film-making and I'd be honored if you would be my intern for the summer."

I nod my head fervently, temporarily rendered speechless.

Oscar is a director of photography and he and I had talked about me being his intern this summer. But never in my wildest dreams did I think Mr. West was going to take me on as his personal intern.

"Thank you," I finally say.

"My pleasure."

And then he turns and leaves.

I want to jump up and down and scream, but I try to keep my composure.

Hunter turns to me and smiles. "Cool."

"Oh, my God, I know."

Then he gives a wicked grin. "You know what this means, don't you?"

I shake my head. "This means you are going to have to spend the entire summer with me?"

I raise an eyebrow.

"I'm working on the set all summer, too."

I can't hide my grin. "Best news ever."

"Right?" he says.

He leads me out on the deck of the penthouse and we lean on the rail looking out at the ocean.

The looming presence of what isn't said seems to hang in the air between us.

There is no more avoiding it. He knows it too.

"Hunter?" It's all I need to say.

He turns to face me. "I accepted the Fulbright."

I had expected to feel devastated. I had thought that my legs would grow weak and I would crumple in despair, but instead, I feel a strange, calming sense of peace spread over me.

"It's only for six months," he says. "And then I can come back here and go to USC with you."

I nod. I'm afraid to say anything else. Six months suddenly feels like a lifetime.

But then I smile. And it's a huge grin. And it's genuine.

"I'm happy for you," I say.

He examines my face and I can see right when he registers that I mean every word. He turns to face me and gently tilts my chin up so my eyes meet his.

"Kennedy Conner, you are my sun, moon, and stars," he says in a husky voice. "I don't know what the future holds, but if I have anything to say about it, you are somehow going to be by my side."

He leans down and kisses me then and the entire world melts away.

When he pulls away, I take both of his hands in mine.

"I don't know what the future holds, either, Hunter," I say. "But every second with you has been worth it."

He looks down at me and for a second his eyes glisten and I wonder if he's going to cry. But then he smiles and takes my hand.

We walk back into the party holding hands and for a second it seems like everyone and everything in the room freezes and the sound disappears. I take in this dream party and hold it close to my heart, capturing the glamorous women in silky gowns, the men in tuxedos, the hundreds of glowing candles, the caviar, the Champagne and chocolate fountain, the movie stars and famous directors. I gaze in wonder at this moment frozen in time.

And then just as quickly, everyone starts speaking and moving again.

Although, it breaks my heart that Hunter is going to accept the Fulbright Scholarship and leave me for at least six months, it also brings me a sense of peace. Because I would never ever ask him to give up his dreams. If he rejected this amazing opportunity just to be with me, I don't think I could live with the guilt.

Knowing that Hunter is pursuing his dreams will be enough for me. I will make it enough.

For now, I will live every moment to the fullest. I will hold on tight to moments such as this night and attempt to memorize every second I get to spend with this amazing boy.

I will tuck these memories deep in my heart and make them a part of me forever.

I don't know what the future will bring. I only know that it will be infinitely better because I am lucky enough to have Hunter West in my life. That may change. But until it does, I'm going to soak up every glorious second I can with this boy I love.

As we walk out, he leans over and whispers in my ear.

"I can't wait to spend the summer with you. Let's make it the best summer of our lives."

And right then, I know that it will be. Nothing can stop us.

THE END

To Be Continued ....

\*\*\*

**Want to read more Hunter and Kennedy?**
**Grab next book in the series, *The Bad Girl*.**
\*\*\*
I hope you enjoyed *The Mean Girl*. If you want to be first to hear information on new books and sales, sign up for my newsletter
https://www.subscribepage.com/ashleyrosebooks
BONUS: If you've read *Raven* (AFTER meets PAPERTOWNS ) and
"This generation's Outsiders."
You'll get the exclusive epilogue to that book so you can find out what happens to Raven & Hazel.
\*\*\*NOT AVAILABLE ANYWHERE ELSE\*\*\*
Remember, You'll also be the first to know when each book in the Pacific High Series is available!
https://www.subscribepage.com/ashleyrosebooks

Printed in Great Britain
by Amazon